Countdown to Easter

Dianna Houx

Copyright © 2023 by Dianna Houx

All Rights Reserved.

No part of this book may be used or reproduced by any means, graphic, electronic, or mechanical, including photocopying, recording, taping, or by any information storage retrieval system without the written permission of the publisher except in the case of brief quotations embodied in critical articles and reviews.

This is a work of fiction. Names, characters, businesses, places, events, locales, and incidents are either the products of the author's imagination or used in a fictitious manner. Any resemblance to actual persons, living or dead, or actual events is purely coincidental.

Contents

1. -Days till Easter- Twenty   1
2. -Days till Easter- Nineteen   11
3. -Days till Easter- Eighteen   21
4. -Days till Easter- Seventeen   29
5. -Days till Easter- Sixteen   39
6. -Days till Easter- Fifteen   49
7. -Days till Easter- Fourteen   59

8.	-Days till Easter- Thirteen	69
9.	-Days till Easter- Twelve	77
10.	-Days till Easter- Eleven	83
11.	-Days till Easter- Ten	93
12.	-Days till Easter- Nine	101
13.	-Days till Easter- Eight	109
14.	-Days till Easter- Seven	117
15.	-Days till Easter- Six	127
16.	-Days till Easter- Five	137
17.	-Days till Easter- Four	145
18.	-Days till Easter- Three	153

19.	-Days till Easter- Two	163
20.	-Days till Easter- One	173
21.	-Happy Easter!-	183
Afterword		193
About the Author		195

-Days till Easter-

Twenty

Grace walked into the town hall/community center and sat beside Molly. "Any idea why Mayor Allen called this 'emergency meeting,'" she asked her friend and business partner.

"Not really," she answered hesitantly. She turned to face Grace and gave her a worried look. "I am concerned, though. There have been rumors floating around for weeks now, and I have a feeling they might be the reason for this meeting."

"What rumors?"

Molly shifted uncomfortably in her seat. At only three months pregnant, she hadn't started to show, but nausea and back pain had become constant companions. "Many older people are unhappy with everything we've been doing these last few months. They feel like we're trying to turn Winterwood into the next Hope Springs and are ruining our town's quiet, peaceful nature."

Grace's mouth dropped open in surprise. "Seriously? But that's the last thing we're trying to do. To sell our small-town experiences, we need our town to stay a 'small town.'"

"I know that, and you know that, but...."

"But they don't know that," Grace finished for her. "Has anyone tried to talk to these people?"

"As far as I know, yes. But it seems to be falling on deaf ears."

"Okay, well, I'm sorry they feel that way, but other than complain, what can they do about it?"

"They petitioned to have your business license revoked. They said your house is not properly zoned for the type of business you're running."

"What?" she gasped. "Why haven't I been told about this?"

"I just found out this morning, and the only reason I know is because Grant was in the mayor's office when it happened."

Mayor Allen entered the room and took his seat in the circle, ending their conversation. Grace sat in stunned silence as the mayor went through the motions of bringing the meeting to order. Her granny had lived in Winterwood her entire life. She had grown up with the people now trying to take away their livelihood. They were her friends and neighbors, and to Grace's knowledge, not one of them had bothered to try talking to Granny first. What they were doing now felt like a betrayal, and if this were the way they would choose to go about things, the town may need to change.

A gentle nudge from Molly brought her out of her daze and Mayor Allen's words into focus. "This morning, my office received a petition to shut down Grace's bed and breakfast business." He paused as an audible gasp erupted from the rest of the council members.

"On what grounds?" asked Mr. Wilkins.

"Nepotism," Mayor Allen stated matter-of-factly.

"Nepotism?" Grace repeated back skeptically. "But I'm not related to you. Or anyone else on the council, for that matter." She looked around the room to see everyone else as confused as she felt.

"No, you're not. But the authors of the petition claim that you are receiving unfair treatment due to your family's name and history with this town."

Grace shook her head in disbelief. "So, what does this mean? Are you revoking my license?"

Mayor Allen hesitated. "At this moment, no. I have forwarded the petition to the town's attorney and am waiting to hear back from him on how best to proceed. However, let's put our current plans for Easter on hold, just in case."

"But we already have reservations booked," Molly objected. "Shutting us down now would cause significant financial harm to Grace and Granny Josephine."

"I will make sure to pass that information along to the attorney as well," he responded, an uncomfortable expression on his face.

"I can't believe this," Grace said out loud to no one in particular.

"It will be okay, honey," Bea, who was sitting on her other side, said as she patted her arm.

Grace turned to Bea, tears in her eyes. "We need the money this business brings in. I don't know what we'll do if they shut us down."

Bea pulled her into a hug. "Let's not worry about that just yet, okay? There's still a chance the attorney could come back and tell us their petition is without merit."

"And if he doesn't?"

"Then we'll figure something else out."

Unsure of what else to do, Grace pulled herself together and nodded. She even tried to give Bea a small smile for good measure.

Mayor Allen cleared his throat. "I know you're all pretty upset right now, and rightfully so. I will get back to you as soon as I have some answers. In the meantime, please keep this to yourselves."

The council members filed out of the community center in small groups of two and three, whispering among themselves. As Grace and Molly got up to do the same, Mayor Allen approached.

"I'm sorry, Grace. I'm sure this feels like a personal attack, but I can assure you it's not. At least not on my part."

"You're right; it does feel personal. I've known these people my entire life. For them to accuse me of trying to throw my family's name around like I'm some social pariah is hurtful at best."

"I don't think they mean it like that."

"Then how do they mean it? We haven't done anything wrong. In fact, my business has done a lot of good for this town. We've brought in a ton of revenue that we would never have seen otherwise for Winterwood and local businesses. How could that ever be a bad thing?"

Mayor Allen reached out and grabbed her hand. "Trust me, Grace; it isn't a bad thing. Most of us are thankful for what you've done, and if it were up to me, I would have ripped up the petition and thrown it in the trash where it belongs."

Grace smiled at the image. "Thank you. I know you're just doing your job."

He gave her hand one last squeeze and then let go. "I'll let you know as soon as I hear something."

The three of them left, Mayor Allen going one way toward his office and Grace and Molly going the other. Once outside, Molly stopped to check her phone. "I got a text from Grant; he wants us to meet him at the hotel."

"The run-down needs to be condemned, that we decided we absolutely are not buying, hotel?

"Yes, that's the one."

"Okaaayyy, why are we meeting him there?"

"I have no idea."

"Really?"

"Yes, really."

Molly started walking toward the hotel. As it was only two blocks from the town hall, driving seemed unnecessary. Grace had to walk fast to keep up with Molly's much longer stride. As a recent Boston transplant, Molly had yet to adapt to Winterwood's much slower pace of life.

When they reached the hotel, Grant was waiting for them outside the front doors with a massive grin on his face. A man Grace had never seen before was standing with him. "What's going on?" she asked suspiciously.

"Grace, Molly, I would like you to meet Bruce Roberts. He's a realtor from Hope Springs."

Bruce gave them each a big smile and took turns shaking their hands enthusiastically. He looked to be somewhere in his mid-twenties, though Grace wouldn't be surprised if this were his first showing as a real estate agent. There was an eagerness to him that she'd never seen in the more experienced realtors around town.

"What's going on, Grant?" Molly asked, echoing Grace's earlier question.

"Bruce here is going to give us a tour of the old hotel," Grant replied excitedly.

"I gathered that. The question is, why?"

"That is something we will talk about later. But, for now, let's see what this baby has to offer."

"Speaking of babies," Grace interjected. "Are you sure it's safe for us to go inside? We've all heard the rumors this place has a mold problem as well as potential structural issues."

"While this place is classified as a fixer-upper, the owner's made sure that all potential health hazards were taken care of before they listed it on the market," said Bruce.

Grace nodded, unsure of whether or not to believe him. As far as she knew, the hotel had sat vacant for around seventy years, which is a lot of time for damage to occur. And, to her knowledge, no one had seen anyone working on the hotel as of late. But curiosity had a way of getting the best of her, so she decided to go with it and follow them inside.

At some point in history, the front entrance had been moved from the corner of the building to the side, likely to accommodate the new street layout. So, the once grand entrance went from two large, double wooden doors under a large canopy to two regular-sized glass doors, similar to those at a gas station. To say it cheapened the look of the hotel would be an understatement.

Since the outside of the building had set the bar pretty low, Grace's expectations for the inside were practically non-existent. So when she walked inside and saw the opulent lobby for the first time, she gasped in surprise, her hand flying to her mouth in shock. She was so enamored with the place that she barely registered Molly grabbing her arm as she, too, looked around in stunned silence.

The ceiling was at least ten feet tall and covered in what looked to be original highly decorative tin ceiling tiles. There were columns strategically placed throughout, likely for structural purposes, but they were also decorative and added to the room's grandeur. A large dark-stained wooden reception desk sat off to one side, and a beautiful crystal chandelier hung in the middle of the room.

The floors had seen better days, the carpet now a raggedy mess that no amount of professional cleaning could save, but that was something that someone could easily replace. It didn't take a lot of effort to imagine the bustling activity that would have taken place in this very room over a hundred years ago. She could easily picture the men and women, in their proper eighteen hundreds style outfits, moving through the rooms or gathering in small groups to discuss the latest news.

She and Molly wandered around as she daydreamed, taking in the sights. Directly off from the lobby was a large room that looked like it might have been a dining room at one time. It had the same ceiling tiles as the lobby, columns lining both sides, and a gorgeous red floor made out of some kind of stone.

"The floor is made out of granite," Bruce commented as he watched them study it. "It's original to the hotel and came from a local quarry."

"Really?" Grace said as she looked at him with interest. "How long do floors like this last?"

"Obviously, over a hundred years," he laughed. "In all seriousness, though, they can last as long as you care for them."

Grace nodded as she took that in. They were in trouble if the rest of the hotel was in as good a condition as these first two rooms. Not only would this place come with a hefty price tag, but the new owner would have no problem getting a hotel business up and running in a part of town already zoned for commercial use. So not only would they be exempt from Grace's current difficulties, they could easily put her out of business. If she ended up allowed to continue her business.

"This is the nicest part of the hotel," Bruce stated as if reading her mind. "The rest needs a fairly substantial amount of work. There are fifteen rooms per floor, for a total of forty-five, and each one needs new paint, carpet, and furniture at a minimum. Also, since this place was built way before indoor plumbing, all the bathrooms are what they call a 'retrofit,' and only a couple of rooms have them. The rest of the rooms share two large, locker-room style bathrooms, two per floor."

"So if we want each room to have its own bathroom...." Grace trailed off.

"Then you will have to undertake some serious renovations," Bruce said as he nodded. "Although, that might not be a bad idea. Since this place has sat empty since the sixties, the plumbing is likely original to the time it was first installed. If it isn't already necessary, an update certainly won't hurt."

"How much do they want for this place?" asked Molly.

Molly's face had taken on an unreadable expression, and her tone had changed to her professional 'work' voice.

To Grace, that could only mean one thing, Molly was seriously interested in buying the hotel.

"The seller is asking fifty-thousand."

Grace's eyes went wide as saucers, and it took everything she had to keep from blurting out a surprised "that's it!" Instead, she watched in silence as Molly addressed Grant.

"I think we need to have a conversation." She looked at Grace. "All three of us."

They thanked Bruce for taking the time to show them the hotel, then walked over to Molly and Grant's office, just across the street from the town hall/community center/fire department. She wasn't sure about Grant and Molly, but she would need time to process everything that had happened that morning. It was way too much in too short a time.

-Days till Easter-

Nineteen

It was officially spring, but that didn't necessarily mean anything in the mid-west. The weather could go from sunny and warm one day to freezing with ice storms the next. Today, however, was sunny and warm, which was a total contradiction to Grace's mood. In her mind, a dark storm cloud followed her wherever she went.

Back from helping her boyfriend, Cole, out with his morning chores, she went to the kitchen to start breakfast, only minutely surprised to see that the usual gang, Molly, Grant, Gladys, and Granny, was already there. Since it was still early for them, Grace could smell a set-up a mile away, especially when it included her favorite breakfast of french toast and bacon. They wanted something; she was sure of it.

"Good morning," Molly singsonged as she handed Grace a plate of food.

"Good morning," Grace grumbled in response. "You guys sure are up and about early. To what do I owe the surprise?"

"Well, obviously, we want to talk about the hotel," said Grant. "I don't want to rush you, but we must make a decision as soon as possible."

"What's the rush?" Grace asked suspiciously.

Grant took a deep breath and let it out. "The same people trying to take away your business license are also interested in buying the hotel."

"I don't understand. Is that why they want to take away my license? To eliminate the competition?"

"I wish it were that simple, but no. They want to buy the hotel so that they can keep any potential investors from re-opening it."

Grace thought about what he said. Fifty thousand dollars was a lot of money to pony up for a property you have zero intention of doing something with. If they were so serious about keeping the town from growing that they were willing to go to those lengths, what lengths would they go to to shut her down? "What exactly is your plan? Should we buy the hotel to keep them from getting it? Does that even make sense for us? If they buy the hotel, and we are allowed to continue with the B&B, they will be doing us a favor."

"And if you're not allowed to continue with the b&b? What then?"

Grace sighed. "I don't know. But I know that even if we bought the hotel, we would have to spend a lot of time and money before we could open again. Any momentum we've built over the last few months would be gone. Besides, part of the charm of staying here is the cozy atmosphere. We would lose that with a hotel."

"That's true, but it would open up other opportunities," said Molly. "With that amount of space, we could host weddings, reunions, and other large-scale events. There's big money in that business."

There was a lot of tension in the air as they each tried to get the other to see their point of view. If it were up to her, this conversation would have waited until after Granny and Gladys were settled in their room for the day. The last thing she wanted was for Granny to get stressed out or worry about money.

"It doesn't hurt to explore all your options, Grace," said Granny. You could test the waters and see what kind of interest you could get from potential brides. Then, depending on what happens with the petition, you could do both the B&B and the hotel.

"I think we need to talk with our so-called friends," Gladys told Granny. "What they're doing is ridiculous and offensive."

"I think you're right. Why don't you kids see what you can come up with, and we'll see if we can put an end to this nonsense."

"That sounds like a great idea," Molly said enthusiastically. "I'm going to head to the office and reach out to some of my contacts. You two," she said, pointing to Granny and Gladys, "Be careful out there. Your friends might not be so friendly when you see them."

"We should bring Ruby," said Granny.

Grace laughed. "While I think she would like that, she's not much of a guard dog."

"It's the perception that counts," Gladys said, pointing to her head with her pointer finger.

"Try to stay out of trouble," Grace said as she tried to hide her smile. She heard her phone ding and checked her messages. When she saw it was from Mayor Allen, her pulse began racing. "The mayor has called another meeting. He says he has news from the lawyer."

"Did he say what the news is?" asked Grant.

"No, just that we need to come down to town hall as soon as possible."

Grant stood up and grabbed his keys and jacket. "Why don't we all go together? I'd like to hear what he has to say myself."

Grace picked up the dirty dishes and carried them over to the sink. She then walked back to the table. "Will you two be okay on your own?" she asked Granny and Gladys.

"Of course, dear. Let us know what happens," assured Granny.

Molly and Grace grabbed their purses and followed Grant out of the house and to the car he had parked by the curb. Too nervous to talk, Grace sat quietly in the back seat, lost in her thoughts. It felt like her entire future was riding on the outcome of this meeting, and to be honest, it was. She would lose almost her entire income if she lost her bed and breakfast. Something like that was tough to come back from. And with her ability to work severely limited by the need to be Granny's full-time caretaker, there were few options on where she could go from there.

***

The three of them walked into the community center, which was one large room attached to the town hall offices. From the looks of it, they were the last to arrive, the rest of the council members already seated and waiting. Mayor

Allen walked in a few minutes later, his demeanor that of a man in a hurry.

"A lot is going on at the moment, so I'm going to make this quick," he stated. "The attorney went through our by-laws and found no reason to terminate Grace's business license." He paused when the room erupted in applause. Then, after a minute of excited exclamations and congratulations, he held up his hand to silence the noise. "That means we will continue our plans for the upcoming Easter celebration. However, I have spoken to the group who created the petition, and to say that they are unhappy with this outcome is an understatement. I will continue my efforts to come to an understanding with them, but in the meantime, I advise all of you to proceed with caution."

"Do you anticipate them causing trouble?" asked Grant, concerned.

Mayor Allen hesitated. "I wish I could say no, but honestly, yes, I do. I am hopeful that they will stay inside the law. However, this is a group of people with nothing but time on their hands...."

"So what you're saying is we should prepare for anything?" Grant asked, although it was more a statement than a question.

"They have already declared an intent to protest at various locations throughout the town, including outside Grace's house. Unfortunately, as long as they remain civil and stay on public property, there's not much we can do to stop them."

"Are you serious?" asked Grace incredulously. "People are allowed to protest in front of my home, and there's nothing I can do about it?"

"It's a gray area," he waved his hand dismissively. "All I can say for now is to be vigilant, and if you come across them, keep to yourself. That's all I have for now. We can start the daily meetings in preparation for Easter next Monday." With that, he left the room as quickly as he came in, leaving them all in stunned silence.

Grace looked around the room at everyone who had come together to help her last Christmas. "How did it come to this," she asked out loud to no one in particular.

"Some people just don't like change, darlin'," shrugged Addie. "I think we should get together and host a dinner for all the disgruntled folks. Remind them that they're part of a community and assure them that we have no intention of turning Winterwood into a big city. Maybe that'll be enough to calm things down."

In Grace's opinion, that seemed unlikely, but she was willing to try. Sometimes it's easier to change people's minds when you force them to face the people they are trying to hurt. Since the weather was still supposed to be nice, they agreed that Grace would host the dinner at her place the following evening. Addie and Bea would help with the food while the rest would provide an assortment of drinks and disposable dinnerware.

Once that was settled, Grace followed Grant and Molly back to their office. They sat in the conference room, Grace slumping in despair. "I can't believe this is happening," she groaned. "Can you imagine how our guests will react if they show up to a group of elderly protesters?"

"Don't worry about that just yet. We still have time to figure things out before that happens," Molly said reassuringly. She reached across the table and patted Grace on the hand.

"Hey everyone, what's going on?" asked Emilio from the doorway. He looked around the table at each of their faces. "Is this a bad time?" he asked uncertainly.

"Not at all," assured Grant. "I'd like you to join us. We could use an outside perspective."

Emilio walked in and sat down next to Grace. She tried to smile at him but couldn't quite pull it off.

"You know that hotel I've been talking about?" Grant asked Emilio. When he nodded, Grant continued. "We need to decide whether to put in an offer. And, unfortunately, we need to make that decision now."

That got everyone's attention, including Grace's. This was the big moment she had been dreading. If they bought the hotel, they risked angering the protesters even more. It could seriously derail their plan to convince them that they aren't trying to grow the town when buying a hotel sends the opposite message. However, it would give them a backup plan and the ability to grow their business. Which still didn't have to equate to growing the town.

If they don't buy the hotel, the protesters likely would, and that would eliminate their options. Plus, it allowed the protesters to compete with them if they decided to take that action. Regardless, she couldn't see a straightforward course of action. And none of that took into consideration the costs involved.

"I've run the numbers and checked out other event spaces in the surrounding areas. From a financial investment standpoint, you should make the purchase. I would be interested in becoming a partner if that is something you would be willing to consider."

All eyes were on Emilio, and all were wide-eyed with their brows raised. It would not have been an exaggeration to say that none of them had expected that response.

Grant sat up straight in his chair. "I feel I should warn you that there are some 'concerns' from some of the residents who may cause some minor problems for us should we proceed."

Emilio smiled. "I am well aware of the current situation. Unfortunately, it's all anyone talks about at breakfast at Addie's. I can assure you that this isn't my first rodeo, nor do I foresee it becoming an issue long-term. There will always be those resistant to change, but if you give them long enough, they usually come around."

"You're welcome to come to the B&B for breakfast," said Grace. "No pressure, though."

"Thank you, I appreciate that and might just take you up on your offer," he said, giving her a warm smile.

"So, have we finally decided?" asked Grant impatiently. "I want to get the ball rolling if we're going to do this." he looked at Grace expectantly, as she was the final holdout.

Grace sighed. "Okay, fine, I agree. I have no idea what you want from me or how any of this will work, but I trust you to figure it out."

Grant's face lit up like a Christmas tree. "You won't regret this," he said as he came around the table and hugged her.

"I certainly hope not," she said, hugging him back. "I need to get back to the house. Call me if you need anything or have any news."

She walked out into the sunlight and stopped on the sidewalk momentarily to bask in the warmth. For now, her business was safe and may even be growing. Yes, there were still problems to address, for right now, she would take the win.

-Days till Easter-

Eighteen

It was almost time for dinner with the protesters, and Grace was more than a little nervous. Granny and Gladys had spent the afternoon the previous day attempting to talk with their now presumably former friends, but none of them had answered their door. When Granny and Gladys relayed their news, they had been close to tears, bringing tears to Grace's eyes. It was hard to believe that the protesters were the same people she went to church with each week.

While she could sympathize with their feelings and understand their right to them, she couldn't understand their current behavior. Their entire group represented less than one percent of the total population of Winterwood. Did they have the right to try to dictate the business of the town? Grace sure didn't think so. She could think of several examples of towns, several of them nearby, that had died out due to beliefs similar to the ones these protesters held. And while she certainly had no desire to see her town grow to the size of Hope Springs, or worse, Kansas City, she didn't want to see it die out either.

Business was essential to a town's survival. The town needed tourists to come and spend their hard-earned money in Winterwood. Local businesses needed it more. Without local job opportunities, people would be forced to seek employment elsewhere, which led to them moving closer to work, which led to fewer people, etc. So, in her opinion, a slight growth wouldn't hurt anyone. But, unfortunately, few people were interested in her opinion.

The doorbell rang the same time the oven timer went off, causing her to jump at the sudden outburst of noise. Fear of burning her tarts caused her to focus on the oven instead of the door, so she was surprised when a pair of strong arms wrapped around her waist. Her tarts placed safely on the counter; she turned around and wrapped her arms around Cole's neck, pulling him close as she buried her face in his chest. "I'm so glad to see you," she whispered.

His deep chuckle rumbled in her ear as he held her tighter. "We just saw each other this mornin', darlin'."

"Yeah, but it feels like an eternity has passed." She pulled back and kissed him, her stress and tension melting away from the heat of his embrace. "How long can you stay," she asked breathlessly when they finally broke apart.

"I'm yours for the night," he replied, kissing her on the forehead.

"But what about the bar?"

"What about it?" he grinned when she rolled her eyes. "Jess and Erin are more than capable of handling things without me for a night. Besides, they have my number if they need me."

"Thank you," she said, relief flooding her body at the thought of having his support.

"You didn't think I would leave you to deal with this alone, did you?"

Grace shrugged. "Between your chores at the ranch and running the bar, you're a busy man. I wouldn't have blamed you if you needed to sit this one out."

He pulled her close to him again. "I'm never too busy for you, Grace. I hope you know that."

Too emotional to speak, she kissed him again, praying that her actions spoke louder than the words she was too choked up to speak. For someone who had spent her life pretty much alone, except for Granny, of course, his support meant the world to her. When they pulled apart, she stared into his eyes, lost in a sea of emotions. "Maybe we should just forget about this dinner and spend the night cuddling in front of the fireplace instead," she said, a dreamy expression on her face.

A sexy grin spread across his face. "You know I'd love nothing more, darlin', but tonight is important. It will be better for everyone if we can get these guys on our side."

"You're right," she said with a sigh. "I just wish we didn't have to do this." She gave him one last kiss and then returned to working on her tarts. In the not-to-distant past, Grace had been considered an absolute failure in the kitchen, but after countless hours of trial and error, not to mention all the hours spent watching how-tos on YouTube, she was now pretty decent, her most requested item, her tarts.

While she finished decorating, Cole went outside to start the barbecue. In an effort to impress, the council members had decided to offer a wide range of food, including chicken, hamburgers, hot dogs, and fish. Molly had taken off work early and had spent the afternoon with Grace stringing lights up around the deck and decorating the tables and chairs. One thing was for sure; the protesters would be unable to claim that no one made an effort. Now they just had to hope they showed up.

The tarts done, she joined Cole outside to help with the meat and found him in a discussion with Grant and Molly. "Sounds like you guys are buying a hotel?" Cole asked Grace, his brow raised in surprise.

"We've put in an offer; nothing is official yet," she replied. She winced when she saw the look on Cole's face. "I guess I forgot to tell you what with everything going on right now. I'm sorry."

Cole remained silent, which in her mind, was worse than him getting angry. She walked over to him, wrapped her arms around his waist, and hugged him from behind. "I'm sorry, I should have told you. We haven't even worked out the details yet, and the issues with the protesters seemed more pressing. I honestly forgot all about the hotel."

He held her arms, returning her hug as best he could in that position. "I'm not mad at you. It just would have been nice to at least be told about a decision that could affect our future."

That surprised her. "In what way does buying the hotel affect our future?"

Cole turned around to face her. "It's a little soon to discuss living together or getting married, but I hope we're moving in that direction. So, all of our decisions, especially big ones, have the potential to affect our future."

Grace shook her head. It could just be her naivete, but she still didn't understand. When he saw the confused look on her face, he tried again. "When we get married, all our debts and assets will be combined. So, if you take on a massive amount of debt, it can negatively affect us both down the road."

Grant cleared his throat. "I don't mean to interrupt, but as the one with the details, I feel like I may be better equipped to answer your questions. Both of yours," he added. "Maybe we should schedule a time later this week to discuss the plans? I feel like we have enough on our plate for the evening."

"That sounds good," Cole agreed, his eyes never leaving Grace's face. "We can talk later, too," he whispered in her ear.

Voices coming from inside caught their attention, and they turned to see that the council members and the group of protesters had arrived. Since she had never seen a copy of the petition, Grace had no idea who the protesters were, so she was more than a little surprised and hurt to see that they truly were people she had known her entire life, whereas before, she had only assumed they were friends of her granny.

Leading the pack was a woman named Dot, who just so happened to be the wife of Roy, Junior's friend and fellow horse and carriage driver. Roy was conspicuously absent, which hopefully meant that he was not a part of his wife's crusade. It would be a real shame if the man that had helped her pull off her Old-Fashioned Christmas Experience decided to turn on her too.

In addition to Dot, Grace counted ten other people. All of them were farmers, and all of them had lived in

Winterwood their entire lives. The most infuriating part was that they all lived outside city limits, so what exactly was their problem? Junior and Bea also fit that description, and they were happy with the town's direction. Cole, too, although he was quite a few decades younger.

After the group got settled, Granny and Gladys appeared, looks of pure disgust on their faces as they surveyed the crowd. "I can't believe my eyes," said Gladys in a voice much louder than usual. "Look at all the backstabbers," she nudged Granny with her elbow. "And to think we go to church with these people every Sunday."

"There ain't no need to be bringin' up church," Dot yelled. "We ain't doin' nothin' but tryin' to protect our town. In my opinion, that's the Christian thing to do." She nodded fiercely as the others echoed their agreement with a loud "Amen."

"I've always thought it shameful to see a person claim to be a Christian right before they do the exact opposite of what Jesus would do," Granny said, staring directly at Dot.

"We ain't here to talk; we're here to eat. So let's get on with it," Dot spat.

"Actually, you're here to do both," Bea said, as she tried to take the diplomatic approach and diffuse the situation. "We would like to take this opportunity to share our plans with you so that you can see that we are not trying to do the things you're accusing."

"There's nothing you can say to change our minds. We've already witnessed what you're doing with our own two eyes. So anything that comes out of your mouths will be lies."

"Then why are you here?" asked Grace. It was painfully clear that their plan had failed. There was no arguing with these people, no chance of winning them over.

Dot shrugged. "We're not stupid. Someone offers us a free meal; we'll take it."

Grace sighed in exasperation. She opened her mouth to respond, but Granny cut her off. "I don't understand how you can act this way toward my granddaughter. You were there all those years ago when she lost her parents. You've been there watching her as she grows up. She's not doing anything wrong, yet you persist in trying to ruin her life. What happened to you, Dot? To all of you? Where did your sense of decency go?"

Dot's eyes narrowed as she listened to Granny. "Don't you try to guilt trip me by bringing up Grace's parents. What happened back then was tragic, but it doesn't give her a free pass to urbanize our town."

"That's not what I'm trying to do!" Grace exclaimed. "We're just trying to bring tourists to the area. We're only doing holiday-related events, which means we aren't even doing this once a month. So there is literally no reason for you to be mad."

"Your first holiday 'extravaganza' caused these two to move here," she said, pointing at Molly and Grant, "And a new business to open up. Your second one brought another man to town. If you keep this up, next thing we know, developers will be out here trying to buy up all our land to build their over-priced subdivisions. We are a farming town; we do NOT want subdivisions."

It wasn't easy, but Grace managed to refrain from bringing up the subdivision that had gone in behind the bank. That little tidbit would have only added fuel to the fire.

Instead, she took a deep, calming breath and tried again. "Look, I don't want that any more than you do. I love our town the way it is. But this town is unable to support us financially. We need money, and that money needs to come from outsiders willing to visit and then leave to return to their homes."

Dot harrumphed and rolled her eyes. "I don't blame you, Grace; you've led a very sheltered life. They don't have the saying 'wisdom comes with age' for nothin'. So do us all a favor and respect your elders, will ya?"

Thoroughly defeated, Grace gave up. There would be no meeting of the minds. No compromises. No parting of ways as friends. At this point, she could only hope that the collateral damage this one-sided war caused would be minimal.

-Days till Easter-

Seventeen

After Grace's confrontation with Dot the night before, the evening had rapidly gone downhill. Granny and Gladys had spent the night glaring daggers at Dot while Dot and the rest of her gang studiously ignored everyone outside their group. They ate as much as possible, then left without so much as a bye-your-leave. It was one of the rudest displays she had ever witnessed, and she had just recently been forced to play hostess to her ex-boyfriend's rich, influencer girlfriend.

Too emotional to sleep, she had gone to Cole's house and had fallen asleep snuggled up in his arms on the couch. They had woken up at five thirty as usual to do the chores and had then spent another hour cuddling before she had to get back to the house for breakfast. Leaving his arms seemed to get harder and harder. Everything truly felt right in the world when she was with him.

When she arrived home, she parked in the driveway at the back of the house and walked over to the side porch to let herself in. As she was walking, she noticed a strange smell in the air that seemed to be coming from the front of the house. Curious, she passed the side porch and continued to the front, only to discover, to her horror, that the entire front of her house was covered in eggs.

The entire front porch, including all the furniture and décor, was covered in broken shells and raw eggs. Slimy eggs dripped down the siding and clung to areas where it had started to dry. They even littered the walkway between the house and the sidewalk. There had to be dozens upon dozens of eggs.

As she surveyed the damage, tears streamed down her face. While egging a person's home has been a known prank for decades, this was not a prank but an act of cruelty, spite, and perceived revenge. Only one group would have a reason to do something like this. And despite their actions the night before, she still couldn't imagine them hating her enough to do something like this.

With shaking hands, she pulled out her phone and called Cole. When he answered the phone, she was so upset her words came out in a jumbled, incoherent mess, so he promised to be over as soon as possible and hung up. That done, she sat on one of the few dry spots to wait, hoping he wouldn't take long.

A few minutes later, Cole came screeching to a halt in front of her house, part of his tire up on the curb. He had barely turned off the engine when he was out of the truck and rushing to her side. "What's wrong? Is it Granny?" he asked, his voice shaken.

Grace shook her head and pointed to the house, his eyes following in confusion. He stood there silently for a few minutes, taking it all in. Then, finally, he let out a low whistle and turned back to look at her, pulling her into his arms when he registered the look on her face. "Are you okay?" he whispered against her ear.

"No." That one word opened the floodgates, and she sobbed in his arms as he held her tightly. She had always been the kind of girl that faded into the background, the type that was ignored and often forgotten. What she was not was the kind of girl that made enemies. Things like this did not happen to her. In fact, the only time she had ever been in a confrontation had been with her ex. And even that was mild compared to this.

Cole held her for a few minutes before he pulled back and handed her his handkerchief to wipe her nose. "Sweetheart, I know you're upset, but we really need to deal with this. The longer it dries, the worse it's going to get."

'Sh-should we call the police?" she stammered.

"Yes, but we can't afford to wait on them. You—"

"Hey, what's going on over here?" asked Grant as he interrupted Cole.

Cole pointed toward the house. "Grant, can you please call the police? And Molly, can you take pictures? We need to get a move on here before this gets any worse."

Grant and Molly stared at the house in silent horror as Gladys shuffled over with her walker. When she saw what everyone was fussing over, she screamed. "HOW DARE THEY! THOSE BACKSTABBING, GOOD-FOR-NOTHING, REDNECK HILLBILLIES!"

The unexpected outburst startled Grant and Molly into action, who took off to complete their respective tasks. Grace, on the other hand, burst into laughter. When she finally got a hold of herself, she walked over to Gladys and draped her arm around her shoulders. "I think you may have just insulted redneck hillbillies," she said as she wiped the tears, this time from laughing so hard, from her eyes.

"I think you may be right," Gladys grumbled. "I'm so sorry, Grace. This is awful."

Grace smiled up at the woman who had long since become a second grandmother to her. As they lamented, the police arrived and surveyed the scene, followed by Mayor Allen. When he approached, Grace felt a renewed sense of anger. "Does this seem the work of law-abiding citizens to you?" she asked angrily as she pointed toward her house.

The mayor hesitated momentarily, then cleared his throat as realization dawned on him. "You think the protesters did this?"

"Unless there's another group of people out there who hate me, I'd say it's pretty obvious who did this."

"But Grace, those people are elderly. They couldn't do something like this."

Grace snorted in the most unladylike manner. "They had no problems coming to my house last night and eating all my food. You act like they're bedridden or something. No sir, those protesters are more than capable of something like this."

He still looked uncertain, but whether that was because he couldn't believe it or didn't want to believe it, only he knew. "Is this going to affect your bookings for Easter?" he finally asked.

Surprised at the question, Grace took a minute to think about it. "We still have a couple of weeks. Why would this affect our Easter plans?"

Allen shrugged. "Eggs can cause a lot of paint damage. So you may need to repaint this part of the house."

Grace's jaw hit the floor. "We don't have the money for that. Besides, the house hasn't been painted in decades; we'll never be able to match the paint color. We'll have to paint the entire house. And have you seen my house? It's huge. Something like that will cost a fortune."

"Insurance might cover it..." he started to say as Cole came around from the back of the house. He was carrying a hose and bucket with some kind of liquid.

"Molly, take Gladys in the house, please. You're going to need to stay inside and away from these chemicals. Grace, we need to get to work." He handed her a pair of gloves and a scrub brush and then proceeded to pull out another set for himself.

The police finished their report, made some empty promises to get back to them if they found the culprits responsible, and then left, taking Mayor Allen with them. Grace was glad to see them go. She was mad at the mayor for the first time in her life and couldn't believe he refused to acknowledge that Dot and her gang of elderly misfits had done this to her house. She deserved better than that from him.

***

Grace and Cole spent the entire morning scrubbing the porch, and everything on it, as carefully as they could to limit the damage as much as possible. It was a long and tedious process that, despite their best efforts to try to make fun, was pretty miserable. Cole, bless his heart, didn't complain once, a claim that Grace herself could not make. If she had to choose between scrubbing eggs off her porch and shoveling horse poop, the horse poop would win every time.

It was lunchtime when they finally finished, so they went inside to clean up. Surprisingly, they still had some leftovers from the night before, along with all of the tarts that Grace had made. Once Dot had declared that she was only there for the food and had no intention of listening, Grace refused to serve her sought-after dessert. In her opinion, they didn't deserve it, and she refused to reward bad behavior.

Once they were cleaned up, they sat down to eat the meal Molly had graciously made for them. "How did it go," Molly asked once they were seated.

"Everything is clean," Grace said between bites. "Some of the paint came off, but at this point, it isn't that noticeable. If we're lucky, we might be able to make it another year or two before we have to repaint."

"That's only if we can keep this from happening again," said Cole. "That paint won't hold up to a second cleaning."

"How do we keep it from happening again?" asked Molly. She was unsettled, although who could blame her? It wasn't every day you went outside to find your neighbor's house covered in egg slime.

"I'm going to go up the city after we finish eating and buy a security camera from the hardware store. We may be unable to stop them, but we can at least catch them." Cole shrugged. "Maybe I'll even put up a couple of signs. That might deter them."

"Or it will make them more careful," Grace pointed out. "If they know we're watching, they can cover their face."

"True, but I'm planning to get the kind of camera that sends an alert to your phone when there's activity outside.

This way, if something happens, you can alert the police right away."

"After the response we received earlier, I'm not holding my breath on the Keystone Cops being much help," Grace said sarcastically.

Cole reached over and grabbed her hand. "It'll be okay." He got up and grabbed his keys off the table. "I'm going to run up there now, so I can get back in time for the evening chores. I'll see you later."

Grace walked him to the door. "Do you want me to go with you?"

"No, you need to take care of things around here. I'll be back in a couple of hours."

She stood on her tiptoes and kissed him as passionately as she dared in the foyer of a house full of people. "Thank you," she whispered.

A slow grin spread across his face as he tipped his cowboy hat to her. Then, with a final kiss on her forehead, he was gone. Grace sighed and returned to the dining room, where Molly was waiting for her.

"We need to talk about Easter," said Molly. While Grace was saying goodbye to Cole, Molly had taken her laptop out to work.

"Please don't tell me you think we should cancel," Grace said with a groan.

"Not at all. In fact, we already have all the rooms booked. There's just one thing."

"Oh no, I don't like the sound of that at all. The last time you told me that, Rebekah showed up. Please don't tell me she's coming back."

"I highly doubt we'll ever see her again," Molly replied dryly.

"Famous last words...." Grace muttered.

"Anyway, we have someone famous coming to stay with us."

That got Grace's attention. She sat up straight in her chair. "I'm all ears."

Molly laughed at the sudden change in her demeanor. "Famous may not be the right word. This guy used to be a child actor. He disappeared from the acting scene after his show got canceled."

"Why is he coming here?"

"Same reason as anyone else," she said with a shrug.

"Do I know who this guy is?"

"I don't know, did you ever watch a show called: Return to Skull Island?"

Grace wrinkled her nose. "No, and that doesn't sound like the name of a children's show."

"It was some adventure show. It was popular for several years; then, the network quietly canceled it. No one knows why."

"Okay, well, is he expecting some kind of special treatment or something?"

"No, but he is coming a week early."

Grace groaned aloud. "What is with everyone always wanting to come early? Ugh, now I will have to entertain this guy for an additional week on top of getting things ready for the rest of the guests. Not to mention that this gives the protesters more time and opportunities to ruin us."

"Hopefully, we'll have all that worked out before he arrives. But, in the meantime, try to focus on the extra money and not the extra work."

"Yeah, yeah, extra money, blah blah..." She got up and cleared the table. It would be nice if the day would come when everything she did wasn't motivated by money. But until that day came, if it ever did, she would have to learn to be grateful for the opportunities that came her way.

-Days till Easter-

Sixteen

Five thirty rolled around way too soon. Not that she was asleep when the alarm went off. Oh no, she was pretty sure she hadn't slept at all. Every single noise she heard was a potential protester back to inflict more damage. And in a house as big and as old as hers, there were a lot of noises. At this point, she would need a lot of coffee to make it through the day.

After a quick trip through the kitchen, where she made the biggest to-go container of coffee she could find, she cautiously approached the front door and slowly eased it open. When nothing jumped out at her, she poked her head out the door and breathed a sigh of relief; the porch was free of eggs. She walked over to the stairs and looked around, but all she could see were shadows. Since it was still too dark to check the rest of the property, she went back inside and locked the door behind her.

Grace had never been physically tortured before, but she was pretty sure psychological torture was just as bad. Not knowing the what, where, and when was driving her crazy.

It had only been a day, but she was already losing sleep and developing a paranoia-based fear of leaving her home. The worst thing is there didn't seem to be anything she could do about it.

Unwilling to let them completely ruin her day, she went to Cole's as planned and, after helping with the chores, spent some time with him before they both had to go to work. There had been a time when the thought of getting up early filled with her dread. But now, she treasured the time those extra hours gave her to spend with Cole, even if she spent part of that time shoveling horse poop.

Back home, she took another walk around the house to ease her worried mind. Now that the sun had come up, she could see clearly, and unfortunately, those earlier shadows now appeared to be giant piles of dirt. Or, on closer inspection, manure. Sighing, she turned around and went inside. She debated checking the cameras but already knew what she would find; nothing. Dot and her gang had been smart enough to dump the manure on the side of the house, away from the cameras. At least the poop was better than eggs.

The question is, what does she do now? She can't just leave two large piles of poop on her lawn. She could call Cole, but he'd already lost an entire day of work the day before when he helped her with the egg fiasco. This was not his war, and he did not deserve to become a casualty of it.

The sound of the front door opening and closing got her attention, and she turned around from the stove just in time to see Grant, Molly, Emilio, and Gladys walk in. "Um," Molly said, a mix of concern and confusion on her face.

"I know," Grace replied with a sigh. "Could have been worse...."

"Did you call the police?" asked Grant. He could always be counted on to see the practical side of things. On more than one occasion, Grace had wished for his ability to set emotions aside.

"No, after yesterday, I decided not to bother."

Grant frowned at her response. "While I agree that they are unlikely to do anything about it, I still think you should call so there'll at least be a record of it. Who knows how far these people are willing to go."

"I guess you're right. I'll call after breakfast." She turned to Emilio. "Glad you decided to take me up on my offer."

Emilio smiled. "Thank you for making the offer."

"How are things going with Vanessa?" she asked as nonchalantly as possible.

"They're going well. We found a great rental in Hope Springs and decided to move in together." He saw the look of surprise on her face and laughed. "Yes, I know it sounds sudden, but it's a duplex, so we each have our own space."

"Things could get awkward if you end up breaking up," Grace pointed out.

"True, but I'm not too worried about that right now. This new arrangement works well and allows us to spend time together since we commute to work."

"Well, I'm certainly no expert in these things," Grace said with a shrug.

"Sorry to interrupt, but what are we going to do with the poo?" asked Molly.

Granny and Ruby appeared in the doorway and walked slowly to the table to sit down. "Manure is an excellent fertilizer," said Granny. "We've talked about planting a garden for years now, Grace; maybe it's time to finally do it."

"I wouldn't mind putting in a few flower beds myself," said Gladys.

Grace raised her eyebrows. "While that sounds like a great idea, I can't imagine a couple of flower beds using all that manure."

"What about a community garden?" asked Emilio. "The park isn't that far from here, and there's plenty of space for a garden. You might even get some of the kids from the school involved to help out."

"I bet a lot of folks around town would be willing to help as well," said Gladys. "Not to mention how upset it would make Dot to see you take something evil and use it for the good of the community."

That would be the best revenge, thought Grace—especially the part where Grace used the manure to beautify her house. Adding beautiful flower gardens would only increase the appeal of the B&B to potential guests. There was just one potential problem. "We'll need permission from Mayor Allen for the community garden."

"Do you think that will be a problem?" asked Molly.

"After the way he acted yesterday, I don't know. I hate to say it, but I don't feel he's on my side right now."

"I'm sure he's just struggling with what to do. This is the first time he has had to deal with something like this," replied Granny. She was always quick with a kind word, something Grace had always admired about her. Hopefully, she was right.

"In that case, I'll call him." That settled, they finished their breakfasts and discussed their plans for the day. There was still no news about the hotel, though Grant assured them that was normal. Grace still wasn't sure about their decision to purchase, so she was unsure what to hope for. If Dot was this angry about her B&B, how would she react to the news that they also bought the hotel? And how far was she willing to go to try to stop them?

***

In a surprising turn of events, for Grace anyway, Mayor Allen had loved her idea to start a community garden. He had called an emergency town council meeting where he called for a vote to set aside an acre of unused space over by the pond. The vote had been unanimous; many council members were avid gardeners. Junior volunteered to bring his tiller into town that afternoon to prepare the ground, and the rest offered to spread the word around. Since the next day was Saturday, they decided to make that the event day. Something Grace was thrilled about since that meant she wouldn't have to wait long to get rid of the manure piles. Once they'd finalized the plans, she called Gretchen, the high school secretary, and asked about potential student volunteers. To her immense relief, Gretchen informed her that the school had a gardening club that needed places to garden. Once Grace shared her dilemma, it was decided that the teens would help at Grace's and Gladys's and the new community garden. Principal Adams was even willing to offer extra credit as an incentive to drum up volunteers.

Grace had first-hand experience working with some of the teens, so she was equal parts thrilled and relieved to have their help. Despite how her morning had started, things were looking up. Proof that good really could come from evil.

By the time the afternoon rolled around, she had acquired a large variety of seeds and had a rough idea of what she wanted to accomplish. It was embarrassing to admit, but a small part of her hoped the kids would have ideas about what to do. As much as she loved flowers, gardening had never interested her, and even she could see that her design skills were sorely lacking.

School let out at three, and by three fifteen, over two dozen students were on her front lawn. Grace had only expected a handful. "Hey, everyone," she called out to get their attention. The kids assembled in front of her and stopped talking. She looked around, surprised to see that Jason, the high school football quarterback, was among the crowd. "You're in the gardening club?" she asked him.

He gave her a goofy, lopsided grin. "Yes, ma'am. Anything to get my hands dirty!" A couple of his buddies bumped his shoulder with theirs while they nodded in agreement.

Grace laughed at their antics. She was sure the real reason Jason and a couple of buddies were there had more to do with the girls, but hey, she'd take any help she could get. Besides, Jason had already proven himself to be an excellent young man with a strong work ethic. They were lucky to have him, regardless of the reason.

"Do you already know what you'd like us to do?" asked Kim, the president of the gardening club.

The plans she had drawn up were over on the porch with Granny and Gladys, who had come outside to enjoy the warm weather and help with supervision. She looked over at them and then back at Kim, a decision forming in her mind. "Tell you what, why don't you guys look at the seeds we bought, and then you come up with a plan."

Kim's eyes went as big as saucers. "You want us to design your new garden?" she asked, awe in her voice.

"Me too," Gladys shouted from the porch.

The girls started squealing in excitement. "I promise you won't regret this," Kim gushed. "We're going to design the most beautiful gardens you've ever seen!"

"I have complete faith in your abilities. Now, while you guys work on that, I will bake some cookies for you." Grace checked in with Granny and Gladys, and seeing that they had everything under control, she went inside to start baking.

As she took the last sheet of cookies out of the oven, she heard yelling coming from the direction of the front of the house. Concerned, she rushed outside to see Dot and co. shouting from the street in front of the house. They were unhappy about the newest turn of events from the sound of it.

Grace had never been quick to anger and preferred to take the diplomatic approach, but watching this group of people, people who had once been considered friends, yell at a group of teenagers was the last straw. She marched across the yard and straight over to Dot. "Can I help you," she asked icily.

"Just what do you think you're doing, young lady? You have no right to..."

"To what?" Grace asked, cutting her off. "To plant a garden in my own yard? You know, it's crazy, I wasn't planning to do a garden this year, but to my surprise, this large pile of fertilizer just appeared on my lawn, and I thought, why not? Don't want to let it go to waste, right?"

Dot was so angry her face turned dark crimson. "I'm taking it back," she sputtered.

"Taking what back?" Grace asked innocently. "Are you claiming that those piles of manure belong to you?"

"You know darn well where that manure came from," Dot spat. Her face went pale when Grace whipped out her phone. "What are you doing?"

"I'm calling the police. You just admitted that the manure belongs to you. Something I think the nice deputy out here this morning would like to know."

Dot stared at her for a couple of minutes as the realization that she had just admitted to a crime came over here. "I admitted to nothing," she finally snapped. "It's your word against mine."

Grace shrugged and put her phone back in her pocket. "Have it your way. If you'll excuse me, I need to get back to work on the garden we're building with my manure."

She turned on her heel, went back inside to get the cookies and lemonade she had made for the teens, and then returned to the front yard. She heard Dot and her followers loudly protesting as she neared the door. When Grace reached the porch, she saw they had lined up on the sidewalk arm-in-arm.

"Anyone have a radio?" she asked as she passed out cookies and lemonade.

Jason's face lit up like a Christmas tree. "I do," he said, smiling mischievously. He put his cup down and ran to his truck, moving it to the side of the house closest to the protesters. Then, he rolled down the windows and turned on a country song as loud as he dared, the bass thumping as it drowned out the chanting.

It was not an ideal atmosphere for planning a garden, the music too loud to hear over, but it was an effective way to shut down Dot. To Grace, that was worth losing a few hours over. Before long, the neighbors came out to see what was happening. Grace watched as a look of triumph came over Dot's face, only to turn to despair when she realized that the neighbors were not there to complain but to join in the fun.

Finally getting the hint that she had lost this battle, Dot left in a huff, taking her posse with her. As for everyone else, the impromptu gathering quickly escalated to a block party, and before long, barbecues were firing up, tables were set up, and food started appearing. They had a blast, all thanks to Dot. Something Grace might have to thank her for the next time she saw her.

-Days till Easter-

Fifteen

You would think that people that had spent their entire lives living in a small town would know that nothing in a small-town stays secret for long. You would be wrong. Dot and her cronies had severely misjudged how the town would react to their crusade.

There may not have been enough proof for the police to make an arrest, but that didn't stop everyone in Winterwood from believing that Dot was responsible for egging Grace's house. They also thought Dot was responsible for the manure piles that had magically appeared in Grace's yard. That made her and her sidekick's persona non-grata at all the businesses in town.

For decades, the farmers had gathered together for coffee and breakfast at Addie's Diner. It may not have always been Addie's, but the tradition had remained the same. Since Addie was not only a council member but one of the business owners that benefited from the tourist activity, she was just as angry with Dot as the rest of them were.

So, effective immediately, Dot and her henchmen were banned from the diner.

To their dismay, Addie was not the only one that banned them. Every business owner in Winterwood, you know, the ones that all benefited from the extra money the tourists brought in, all refused entry to their businesses. This meant that Dot and her comrades were forced to drive forty-five minutes to the big city they hated every time they needed to buy something.

Grace almost felt sorry for them until she remembered all the eggs they had wasted egging her house. Now, she hoped they were forced to buy eggs at the same exorbitant prices the rest of them had to pay while driving to the city to boot.

Saturday had dawned warm and sunny, a perfect day for gardening. To ensure that Dot didn't come back in the middle of the night to take back the manure, Junior had brought his tractor over and moved most of the poop to the park, leaving just enough for Grace's and Gladys's gardens. To her immense relief, not only had Dot left the piles alone, there were no other surprises either. Did that mean they had given up? Unlikely, but at least she was getting a slight reprieve.

Word had spread like wildfire about the new community garden, thanks in part to Molly's posts on the town's social media sites. In true Winterwood fashion, not only had the citizens shown up in droves, they brought enough food to feed an army and turned planting day into a party. For her part, Grace stayed behind to supervise the garden club's efforts at her house. People wandered back and forth, helping where needed and ensuring everyone had plenty to eat and drink.

By the end of the day, the gardens had been planted, fertilized, and watered—flowers at Grace's and Gladys's, fruits and vegetables at the park. The garden club had agreed to maintain the garden at the park as part of their club duties, with a bit of help and supervision from some of the locals.

Once the work was done, the adults headed down to Cole's bar to have a drink and continue the party. They packed the place and turned it into a standing room only, some of them spilling out onto the patio outback. Since she felt partly responsible, Grace went down to help. She couldn't make the drinks, but she was more than capable of serving them.

"You should consider adding some tables and chairs to the patio out back," she said to Cole once she could stop for a minute.

"Yeah, that sounds like a good idea. Any reason why Ted never did that?"

"I'm not sure," Grace said, shrugging her shoulders. "I never came in here when Ted owned it. We could ask around, see what some customers have to say."

"Sounds good to me." He went back to bartending as Grace hurried off to take orders at the end of the bar. When she reached her usual spot, the end closest to the door, she saw Evie and Cassie, friends she used to go to school with, sitting there.

"Hey guys," said Grace. "What can I get you?"

"Got any wine?" asked Cassie. "I feel like wine is in order after a day like today."

"We should have a couple of bottles in the back. Red or white?"

"Red, definitely," replied Evie.

Grace left to get their wine and returned a few minutes later with a bottle and two glasses. "I don't think I've seen you guys in here before. Is this your first time?"

Evie looked down at her lap sheepishly. "We used to go to the other bar, but I no longer feel comfortable showing my face there."

Grace looked at her in surprise. "Why, what happened?"

"I'm sure you heard the rumors surrounding my wedding...." Evie trailed off as Grace winced in response. "I ended up in the other bar right after that fiasco took place, and let's just say I made quite the scene."

"Oh no, they didn't kick you out, did they?" Grace asked, compassion in her voice. She was confident there wasn't a man, woman, or child alive that hadn't heard about Evie's fiance ditching her at the altar for her sister.

"No, they didn't kick us out. But it did get pretty uncomfortable in there, especially after I told everyone all the sad, pathetic details. Of course, it didn't help that we got drunk on margaritas."

"Well, it's hard to believe that anyone would judge you after something like that, but we're glad to have you here," Grace reassured her. "Out of curiosity, what ended up happening with your sister? Unless you'd rather not talk about it?" Grace added hurriedly.

"She ended up marrying Greg out at my parent's farm. A couple of months later, she got pregnant, and then a couple of months after that, she caught Greg cheating on her with one of her friends and kicked him out."

"Oh," Grace said, "That's too bad...."

"Yeah, I've heard it's been a roller coaster. But, luckily, I got off the train to crazy town a while ago, so I'm no longer in danger of getting caught up in the wreckage that will surely occur when that train finally derails."

"Amen to that," Cassie said, raising her glass in a toast. "Here's to the end of toxic relationships and the beginning of healthy ones."

Evie clinked Cassie's glass with hers while Grace looked on in curiosity. "Are you dating someone new?" she finally asked when her nosiness got the best of her.

"Yeah, I'm dating a guy named Jake. He has a cabin out here by the lake."

"Oh, we know Jake. He comes in here on weekends sometimes. He seems like a good guy."

"Who's we?" Cassie asked, her perfectly manicured brow raised.

"Cole and I," Grace said, pointing in Cole's direction.

"You're dating Mr. Tall, Dark, and Sexy?" asked Evie, her eyes wide.

"Yes," Grace replied self-consciously. Her old fears of not being good enough surfaced with a vengeance, so she quickly excused herself to help other patrons as far away from those two as she could.

Evie and Cassie had always been friendly to her, but they had never been close friends. Evie and Cassie had been cheerleaders, while Grace had been a shy bookworm that spent most of her time hanging out in the library. Two very different social circles that never overlapped.

Once the door to her inner pain was opened, her feelings came rushing out like someone had opened a floodgate. She did her best to ignore them, but it soon became too much, and she found herself in the back room trying to dry her tears as fast as they fell. It was too busy out there, and she did not have time to wallow in self-pity. Nor did she want anyone else to see her cry.

A few minutes later, the door opened, so she quickly turned her back and tried to look like she was busy searching for something. Instead, two strong arms wrapped around her from behind, causing the tears that finally dried up to fall again.

"What's wrong?" Cole whispered in her ear.

Grace shook her head. "Nothing, I'm fine," she whispered back.

"Please don't lie to me. I know you, Grace, and you are definitely not fine."

She turned in his arms and buried her face in his chest. "Okay, you win; I'm not fine. But I'm trying to be, and hopefully will be in a couple of minutes."

He ran his hands over her back in soothing motions. "You didn't answer my question."

"Later, okay? There's a lot of people out there, and we do not have time for this."

"I told you I would always make time for you, darlin'. And this is me, making time for you."

Grace smiled up at him. "And I love you for that," she said, her mouth dropping open as she realized what she had just said. They had only been dating for a little over a month. Neither of them had uttered those words to each other before, and while she did mean them, she didn't want to be the first to say them.

The sexy grin she loved so much broke out across his face. "Did you say that 'cause you mean it, or 'cause you're tryin' to distract me?" he drawled.

Now was her chance to back out of saying those words first. But she couldn't do it. The words meant too much to her, and now that she'd said them, she couldn't bear to lie and take them back. "I meant them," she said with a sigh.

"Grace," he put his finger under her chin and gently raised her face to look at him. "Why are you upset?"

"I'm not upset; I'm embarrassed."

"You're embarrassed to love me?"

His grin had changed into a frown, his eyes full of hurt. She was doing a bang-up job of messing things up. "I am not embarrassed to love you. I'm embarrassed to be the one to say it first. I don't want to creep you out or put you on the spot. We've only been dating a month and—"

Before she could finish her sentence, his lips were on hers in what could only be described as an earth-shattering kiss. When he let her go, they were both breathing heavily, and she swore the temperature in the room had risen at least ten degrees. "That was...wow," she said breathlessly.

He framed her face with his hands and stared deeply into her eyes. "I love you, too," he said softly.

"Now, will you please tell me what had you cryin' in my stock room?"

"It doesn't matter anymore. Nothing matters except that you love me," she pulled his face back down to hers and kissed him again. At some point, he would make her talk to him. And at some point, she would be ready to. She seemed incapable of trusting herself, but maybe trusting him was enough.

"Hey, you two," Erin said as she opened the door and peeked her head into the room. "I'm sorry to interrupt, but it's getting pretty crazy out here. We could use your help."

"We'll be right there," Cole replied, his eyes never leaving Grace's. "Guess we better go," he said to Grace.

"Maybe we can pick up where we left off later?' she asked hopefully.

"You can count on it."

They walked out of the room hand-in-hand, separating once they reached the bar area. A glance down to the end of the bar showed that Evie and Cassie appeared to be getting ready to leave, so Grace busied herself on the other side of the bar. Her back turned; she didn't see them come up behind her; her only indication that they were there was a light tap on her shoulder.

Expecting to see another patron, Grace turned around, pen and pad in hand, only to stop short when she saw it was them. "Do you need something?" she asked.

"Hey, I didn't mean to offend you back there," Cassie said apologetically. "I was just surprised to find out Cole had a girlfriend. He's been a friend of my brother's for years and had pretty much sworn off women for good after his divorce."

"It's okay; I shouldn't have taken it so personally. I guess it's just a bit of a sensitive subject for me. I still can't believe that I'm dating him!" Grace tried to laugh, but a strangled sound came out instead. Hopefully, it was too loud in there for them to have noticed.

"Listen, we should all get together and hang out sometime," said Evie. She had to shout to be heard over the crowd.

"That sounds good; how about next weekend?" asked Grace. There had been many instances throughout her past where people had claimed to want to get together, only never to follow through, so she might as well find out if this was another one of those cases.

"Saturday night works for me," Evie replied. "I'll stop by later this week, and we can finalize our plans.

Okay, maybe she meant it. Grace agreed and then went back to serving drinks as fast as the bartenders could make them. When the bar finally closed, she was so tired she practically crawled home and into bed, where, for the first time in days, she finally got a good night's sleep.

-Days till Easter-

Fourteen

When exhaustion hits, it hits hard. The events of the last couple of days had finally caught up to her, and she had slept like the dead through her five-thirty alarm and the security alarm alerts. When she finally woke up, it was nine o'clock on Sunday morning. This meant that not only had she missed helping with the morning chores, but she had also missed the early morning Church service. Although considering that was also the service Dot attended, maybe that wasn't such a bad thing.

After a quick apology text to Cole, who responded that he, too, had overslept, she hurried downstairs to check the front of her house. When she reached the foyer, Molly called out from the dining room. "You don't want to go out there," she growled.

Grace paused at the sound of Molly's voice. She had only known her for four months, but in that time, she had never heard her friend get angry, not even when she was fighting with Grant. "How bad is it?" Grace asked with a defeated tone.

"There are no words," Molly replied. "Come have breakfast first. You'll need your strength, and once you step outside those doors, you'll lose your appetite."

That got her attention. A war waged inside as her curiosity to see what on earth had gotten Molly all riled up fought with her desire not to upset her friend further. Ultimately, the latter won, and she went to the kitchen, grabbed a plate, and sat down across from Molly. "Where's Grant?" she asked between bites.

"Outside talking to the police. I hope you don't mind, but Grant thought he might get a different response than the ones you've been getting...."

Grace's eyes narrowed as she thought about that. "Oh, because he's a man?"

Molly sighed. "Not just a man, a high-powered man from Boston. I've seen this too many times over the years. Women like us get ignored, while people tend to fall all over themselves to help people like Grant. He is not the kind of man people say no to."

"Then I'm glad he's on my side. This whole experience has been very frustrating. As far as I know, the police haven't even talked to Dot, despite everyone else in town knowing she's behind all these 'pranks,'" Grace said in disgust. "It's like they don't care."

"I'm not sure what the problem is, but their refusal to do something is starting to feel personal. No one should have to be subjected to this kind of behavior."

"It's that bad, isn't it?" Grace asked. She held her breath as she waited for Molly to respond. The manure had become a blessing in disguise, but the eggs had been a nightmare. Whatever was going on outside appeared to be even worse than that, although Grace had a hard time imagining what that could look like.

"I'm afraid it's worse," Molly said sadly. "If we can't get this under control, I think we're going to have to cancel the Easter event."

Grace's eyes went wide. "Oh no, please don't say that. Canceling the event will ruin us."

Tension hung in the air, so thick you could cut it with a knife. Molly seemed lost in thought, her silence deafening as panic rose in Grace's chest. Then, as if sensing her friend's distress, Molly grabbed her hand. "Let's see how things go over the next few days, okay?"

It took a lot of effort, but after taking several deep breaths, Grace managed to somewhat calm her nerves. "I'm ready to go outside."

Molly looked at Grace's plate and, seeing that it was empty, nodded. They both got up and walked to the front door. When they reached it, Molly stopped and grabbed Grace's hand. After one last compassionate look, she opened the door, and they walked outside.

The first thing that Grace noticed was the smell. If she had to describe it, the first word that came to mind was landfill. It literally smelled like someone had taken a year's worth of the smelliest, moldiest, foulest trash and dumped it in her front yard. Because...they did. Her once beautiful front lawn was now a sea of garbage, and it didn't stop there. Trash littered her front porch, piled high in her chairs and on top of the tables. It flooded into the side yard and covered the new flower beds they had spent so much time and effort planting. Someone had even stuffed it into her mailbox.

That wasn't even the worst of it. As Grace carefully picked her way down the steps and looked around, she saw that the word 'trash' had been spray-painted on the side of her house. She had been right when Molly told her there were no words. Grace couldn't have strung a sentence of two words together if her life depended on it. The trash could be picked up. It would probably take her all day, but it could be done. The spray paint, on the other hand, was an entirely different story. How was she supposed to deal with that?

As she stared at the wall, Grant and a local police officer approached. "Grace, Officer Smith needs you to give a statement."

"What's the point?" asked Grace bitterly. She turned to stare at the officer, anger flashing in her eyes. "I've already given you a statement two other times, and here you are, back for round three. Talking to you is a waste of time."

"Grace," Grant said softly. "I know you're angry, but we need to follow protocol."

"Is he following protocol?" Grace waved her hand in Officer Smith's direction. "How many leads have you followed so far?" she asked him. "How many suspects have you interviewed?"

"Ma'am, I—"

"None, right?"

When he didn't respond, she shook her head in disgust. "Just as I thought. Wouldn't surprise me to find out you're protecting the old witch," she spat.

His eyes went wide at the accusation. "Now see here," he started to say, but she cut him off.

"No, you see here." Grace stepped closer to him and stuck her finger in his face. "So far, my home has been vandalized three times, and the only thing you have done all three times is take a statement. Unless you're interested in Winterwood turning into the Hatfields and McCoys, I suggest you finally do something, starting with hauling Dot and her underlings down to the station."

Officer Smith took a step back. "I can't just arrest people based on gossip and rumors."

"My granny has lived in this home her entire life and has never had a problem until now. Why now, you might ask? Or should ask. Well, let me tell you. Because some lunatic has decided that she doesn't like that we opened a B&B. Not only did that lunatic file a petition with the mayor's office, giving you her full name as well as the names of her minions, but that lunatic has been all over town crying to anyone who will listen. In fact, I have a large group of witnesses who saw them here Friday."

"Wait, there are witnesses who can place her here after the manure incident?"

"Yes, she showed up while the garden club from the high school was here. I'm not sure how much they heard of the conversation Dot and I had where she admitted that the manure was hers, but they definitely witnessed Dot and the rest of her merry-men link arms and chant at us. My neighbors saw it too."

"Well, that might change things. If you can get me a list of all the people you say witnessed this event, I will start taking statements. It might not be enough to warrant an arrest, but it could be enough to at least haul her down to the station. Sometimes that's enough to curb this kind of behavior."

"I doubt it," Grace said with a snort. "I don't know what it will take to end her reign of terror, but Dot seems to have the stamina and wherewithal of a teenage vandal. Someone this deranged," Grace waved her hand at the mess, "Is unlikely to be deterred by a trip to the police station."

"You're probably right, but I'll do my best. Maybe the threat of spending her golden years in prison will give her some much-needed perspective."

"We can only hope. If you can give me a few minutes, I'll get that list for you." Grace walked away without waiting for a response, gingerly picking her way through the trash as she went. When she got to the porch, she saw Molly still standing there. "You should go back inside. It's not safe for you out here."

"I'm pregnant, not an invalid," Molly said defiantly.

"The smell is terrible, and you have no idea what is in all these piles. This is no place for a pregnant woman. Or for guests...." Grace said sadly.

Molly grabbed her hand again and held it as they waded through the trash to the front door. "I guess you're right. I should probably take care of Granny and Gladys anyway. They're both pretty upset."

"I appreciate that. Please keep them both inside. Does the trash go around to the back of the house? I didn't even look."

"It's only in the front where it's visible from the road."

Once inside, they went their separate ways, Molly to the back of the house where Granny and Gladys were, Grace upstairs to her room to make the list. If she was lucky, she might finally catch a break, but at this point, she highly doubted it. For now, she needed to focus on cleaning up the mess.

When she got back outside, she saw Cole's truck parked at the curb on the side of the house. She heard voices coming from that direction, so she waded through the garbage until she spotted Grant, Cole, and Officer Smith huddled over what looked to be Cole's phone. They appeared to be watching something intently on the small screen. "What's going on, guys?" she asked when she reached them.

"We're watching video footage from last night," Cole replied absentmindedly.

"Do you see anything?" she asked curiously. She wished she could see what they were looking at, but there wasn't enough room for her to squeeze between them.

The guys remained silent for a couple of minutes, and then Cole put his phone away. "We saw the whole thing. But, unfortunately, they were smart and wore ski-type masks that covered their hair and faces," said Cole.

"What about body-type analysis?" she asked hopefully.

"Ma'am, we're just a small-town police department, not the FBI," said Officer Smith.

"You can't send the footage out?"

"For a murder, yes; for something like this, probably not."

A noise broke the silence. It sounded like a cross between a bird and some other kind of animal. Grace looked around and finally spotted some trash rustling over by the porch. "Do you guys see that?" she asked as she pointed to the movement.

"Could be a raccoon or a possum," Officer Smith said with a shrug.

"Well, one of you needs to look," she said as she gave each of them a look.

Cole grinned at her and walked over to the porch. He pulled a pair of work gloves out of the back pocket of his jeans and put them on, then proceeded to gently push the trash out of the way until he exposed a small, white blob of fur. "Awww," he said. "Come here, you little cutie-pie." he scooped up the fur ball and brought it to Grace.

"It's a kitten," she said, taking the animal from him and snuggling it against her chest. "How on earth did a kitten end up in this mess?"

"Looks to me like a Maine coon kitten," said Cole. "Doesn't Dot breed Maine coons?" he asked Officer Smith.

Officer Smith shrugged. "I think I may have heard something about that."

"Since the cat was dumped on my property with the rest of this trash, does that mean I get to keep it?" asked Grace.

"I'm not an expert on the law, ma'am. For that, you might want to consult a lawyer. But in my opinion, for Dot to get the kitten back, she'll have to admit to dumping all this trash. So, it seems like you win regardless."

"Guess I found my silver lining, then."

Officer Smith left, presumably to take statements from the list of witnesses Grace had handed him. Grace took the kitten inside and handed her over to Molly, who volunteered to bathe her and take care of her while Grace was outside. Cole and Grant, bless their hearts, got out trash bags and shovels, and the three of them set to work cleaning up the massive mess.

A couple of hours later, while they were taking a break for lunch, they heard a noise coming from the front of the house. When we went to investigate, they discovered Dot rifling through the piles of trash. "Well, isn't this a surprise," said Grace. "Have you decided to return to the scene of your crime, or are you here to volunteer to help us clean up this mess?"

Dot gave her a dirty look but kept digging. Fed up with her nonsense, Grace approached her. "You are trespassing, ma'am. You have ten seconds to get off my property before I call the police."

"I'm looking for something."

"Ten, nine, eight—"

"Okay, fine," she said as she hurried over to the sidewalk.

"I can't imagine why you would dig through my trash, Dot. Did you leave some incriminating evidence behind?"

"I don't have to put up with this," she muttered.

"No, you don't. You are free to leave. And I suggest that you do it before Officer Smith comes back. I'm sure he'll have the same questions I do."

"This isn't over," she said, but she turned around and returned to her car, which was all Grace could hope for at that time.

Grace turned back to face the guys. "Guess she discovered her kitten is missing."

"Luckily, I recorded a video of her digging through the garbage. At some point, we're going to get enough to finally nail her," said Cole, a triumphant gleam in his eye.

"And I get a free kitten. Not bad for a day's work, Dick Tracy!"

Cole playfully swatted her rear as they laughed at her lame joke. It was late evening by the time they finished picking up the trash. There were at least thirty bags, full to bursting, sitting on the side of the road for trash day. Grace would have to call and ask for a special pick-up, which was just one more expense this woman had cost her.

Even with the trash gone, it still stank. The porch, including the furniture, needed a good washing, and there was still the issue of the spray paint. Two things she was going to have to put off until tomorrow. With only five days to go until her first guest arrived, making the place presentable again would take a miracle. And that was if there were no more 'surprises.'

-Days till Easter-

Thirteen

It had been another sleepless night for Grace, who had snuggled with the kitten while staring at the security app on her phone. Since she still hadn't finished dealing with the latest nightmare, she absolutely could not afford to take another hit. Which left her no other choice than to assume guard duty.

When her alarm clock read five thirty, she sighed heavily and got up, careful not to disturb the sleeping kitten. She had a dilemma. She was sure that Dot and her coterie had shown up to egg her house while she was at Cole's. So that meant, if she left now, she was leaving her house unguarded during a vulnerable time. But, if she chose to stay, she felt like she was letting Dot win. Dot had already cost her so much; losing her time with Cole was just too much to bear.

That decided she got up, dressed, gently picked up the sleeping kitten, and went downstairs, placing her in the dog bed with Ruby. Ruby, a recent mama herself, had taken to the kitten like fish to water, so Grace had no problem leaving the adorable fur ball in her capable paws.

Some may feel like Grace was in the wrong for keeping the kitten; after all, she was Dot's property. But, as far as Grace was concerned, those people could shove it. Grace didn't go to Dot's farm and steal her kitten; Dot came to Grace's and dumped the kitten along with thirty bags of trash. Dot had cost Grace so much time and money, not to mention sleep, that at this point, the cost of the kitten was a drop in the bucket. A meager down payment on a debt she could never repay. The irony was that even the kitten had cost her money.

When she got back from Cole's, she walked the property again, just to make sure, careful to breathe through her nose as she neared the front of the house. Trash day couldn't come soon enough. Luckily, nothing out of the ordinary appeared. Had losing her kitten given Dot pause, or was she busy planning something even more nefarious? Not knowing truly was the worst part.

The daily planning meetings for the upcoming Easter event had begun that morning, but Grace had decided to skip it. She was too tired, had too much to do, and was still pretty upset with Mayor Allen. Was that fair? She wasn't sure. From a logical standpoint, there was little he could do about the Dot situation. But from an emotional standpoint, Grace had expected a lot more concern and compassion from the man she had known for over twenty years, and denying that Dot was involved when it was obvious that she was, was not Grace's idea of concern or compassion.

Since Molly had agreed to go and represent them both, Grace felt confident that she wouldn't miss out on anything important. So, her morning was now free to tackle the horrid mess that was her front porch. Again. Only, this time she was alone.

Determined to get this done as quickly as possible, she put in her earbuds and scrubbed every inch of every surface. By the time she was done, the porch practically sparkled. Too bad that was the easy part. With that done, it was time to move on to the spray paint.

During the night, when she was attempting to stay awake, she researched how to remove spray paint. There were several recommendations, but unfortunately, all of them had the potential to cause damage to the surface she was trying to clean. Not to mention the likelihood of removing the paint she wanted to keep in addition to the paint she didn't. Since her house was old and covered in asbestos shingles, damaging them did not seem like the smart way to go. Which left her with one option: paint over the spray paint.

It was unlikely that even the best paint store would be able to get an exact match, but her house was a dark gray, so somewhere in the ballpark might be good enough. A couple of trips to the hardware store later, she was in business. She feathered on the paint, another tip she learned from her midnight searching, and painted the entire bottom half of that section of the house.

Up close, if you knew to look for it, you could tell that some painting had been done, but far away, she'd be willing to bet that no one would ever notice. Since she still had quite a bit of paint left over, she decided to go over the spots on the porch that had been damaged during the egg fiasco. By the time she was done, she felt pretty proud of herself. The house looked better than it had in decades. Maybe she should be thanking Dot instead. After all, if it weren't for her, Grace never would have made these improvements.

She went inside to check on 'her girls' and found Granny and Gladys in the living room laughing at the kitten chasing toys while playing with Ruby. "I think you've found the fountain of youth," Gladys said with a wink.

Grace smiled. "Looks like Ruby agrees."

"She's been having a blast playing with the new kitten. I feel bad that we gave away all her puppies," said Granny.

"I do too. I planned to keep one of them, but the response to my ad was crazy. Before I knew it, they were all gone."

"Well, none of that matters now," Granny said as she waved her hand. "We need to name this little one, though."

They watched as the kitten did another running jump over Ruby's paws, making cute little meowing noises as she went. "How about Piper?" asked Grace.

"That is such a cute name," said Gladys.

"Oh, I agree," said Granny.

"Then Piper it is." Grace watched the kitten play for a few minutes, then excused herself to make lunch. She could hear Granny and Gladys laughing all the way in the kitchen, which caused her smile to grow so big her mouth hurt. Oh yeah, she definitely owed Dot a thank you.

***

A little after two o'clock, Grace received a text asking her to come to Grant and Molly's office. On her way out the door, she was greeted by a large man in a construction hat and bright orange vest. Startled, she stepped back into the house and half closed the door, ready to slam it shut if necessary. "Can I help you," she asked. It might be a little paranoid on her part to be afraid of a construction worker, but after everything she'd been through the last several days, all strangers that appeared uninvited gave her cause for concern.

Other than the strange look he gave her, he seemed unbothered by her reaction. "Just letting you know we're ready to start the job. Are you sure you want to gravel your entire front lawn?"

"What?" Grace asked, sure she must have misheard him.

The man held up a clipboard with some paper on it. "The lady gave me explicit instructions to gravel over the entire front lawn. I mean, we can do that; I just want to make sure that's really what you want. I mean, once it's done, there are no takebacks, you know what I mean?"

"No, I absolutely do NOT want you to gravel over my front lawn," she responded large emphasis on the word not. "Who told you to do this—never mind, I know exactly who told you." Grace shook her head. Will that woman ever give up? "I'm sorry you wasted your time coming over here, but we will not be needing your services."

"Makes no difference to me," he said with a shrug. "Job's already been paid in full." He looked around a little bit and then turned back to her. "Is there anywhere you might like the gravel? We could add some to your driveway in the back or create another driveway between your house and the neighbors. Looks like that's unusable space anyway on account of the trees."

"We could do that?" Grace asked cautiously.

"Why not?" he shrugged again. "I'm here, gravels here. Might as well make the best of it."

"What happens if the lady that paid you gets mad when she sees you put in a driveway instead of turning my lawn into a rock garden?"

"That's a whole lot of not my problem. Especially when you consider that the lady in question just opened me up to a huge lawsuit by trying to use me in whatever it is you two got going on. She'll be lucky if I don't sue her."

"I do apologize for that. As you can see, she has a major vendetta against me. One that seems to be continuously getting worse. If you don't mind, I would love a driveway on the side of the house."

He gave her a salute and then returned to his dump truck, which was indeed filled with gravel upon closer inspection. Grace could not believe the nerve of Dot. If she had succeeded in her latest scheme, she would have graveled right over the lawn, the walkway, and even the new flower beds. It would have looked horrible and, as the guy said, would have been nearly impossible to undo.

The entire process only took the guy about twenty minutes. He backed up to the end of where the new driveway would go and then slowly drove forward as the gravel spilled out of the back. When that was done, another guy, parked out of sight on the side of the house, came around in a tractor and tamped down the rock. It wasn't the cleanest job in the world; gravel spilled everywhere, but it looked like a driveway and would get the job done. Thanks to Dot, her guests would now have an extra space to park in.

As the guy got ready to leave, Grace ran up to him to ask a couple of questions. "Any chance the woman you spoke to gave you her name?"

"I'm afraid not. She paid in cash, too, so no help there either, I'm afraid."

"That's what I was afraid of. Well, thanks for the new driveway." Grace tipped him with a couple of twenty's and then waved to the other guy as they left.

A text asking where she was came in, so she hurried to her car and drove to the office. If she were lucky, she would make it home in time to see Dot's reaction because she knew there would be a reaction.

She walked in the door to find Grant, Molly, and Emilio waiting for her in the conference room. "What took you so long?" asked Molly.

Grace told them the gravel story. "Will that woman ever learn?" asked Grant. He shook his head.

"From a financial perspective, she is making one bad decision after another."

"Is her bank account really the only thing we care about?" Grace asked drily.

"Of course not, it's just—"

Grace waved her hand in Grant's direction. "It's fine, Grant. I know old habits die hard. So, what's going on?"

"They accepted our offer," Molly exclaimed excitedly. She was so excited she was practically bouncing in her chair.

"Wow, we're really doing this." Grace still wasn't sure how to feel about buying the hotel. All of her earlier concerns were still valid. The only thing that had changed was they now had a mortgage payment to add to the mix. "Do you know if Dot ever put in an offer?"

"Um, three other people put in offers in addition to ours. The realtor was not allowed to tell us the names of the other buyers, but he didn't deny it when I asked if Dot was one of them," replied Grant.

"So if we're just finding out that our offer's been accepted, that means that she's finding out hers has been rejected...." Grace trailed off. If Dot was angry before, she was going to be livid now. Grace started to fear that it might never be safe to sleep again.

-Days till Easter-

Twelve

Another sleepless night had passed uneventfully. Which was either good or bad; Grace could no longer tell. There were only four more days until her first guest arrived, and she desperately needed to get the house in order and start decorating, but she was terrified to do so with Dot still on the loose. But if she didn't start soon, she would have a very disappointed guest on her hands.

Once daylight was in full bloom, and she felt relatively safe from Dot's antics, she took off for the city to shop for Easter decorations. She was looking for a mix of cute for the kids and classy for the adults, with some Spring décor thrown in for good measure. One of her favorite parts of running a B&B was decorating. She loved seeing her beautiful home transformed into something magical.

Back home, Granny and Gladys came out to watch and keep her company as she moved around the house, adding decorations to practically every surface while Piper followed behind, checking out her new 'toys.' It would be challenging to keep the curious kitten away from the décor, but Grace was pretty sure the guests would be willing to overlook her mischief once they saw how cute she was.

Speaking of guests, Conor McBride, the former child actor, was due to arrive in four days. His room was ready, and with any luck, the house would be too, but she had no idea what she would do with him when he arrived. None of the activities the council was planning would take place for at least a week, and it's not like they lived in an area with a lot of entertainment opportunities. She supposed she could invite him to hang out with Cole, Evie, Cassie, and Jake. That would at least take care of Saturday night, but what about the rest of the week? Something to think about.

The rests of their guests were all families with elementary school-aged kids and younger looking for a fun holiday vacation. They would be easier to entertain since most of their activities would focus on the children. Grace would, of course, offer some adult activities for after the kids went to bed, but those would consist of games and drinks, none of which would be fun for one guy. Hopefully, this would be the last time Molly booked a guest to arrive earlier than the agreed-upon date.

It took all afternoon, but inside, the house was completely transformed. Grace briefly contemplated starting on the outside but decided to leave that to the last minute, just in case. She could just imagine waking up the following day to find that Dot and the rest of the insurgents had snuck back onto the property and destroyed it all. Not that she'd actually be sleeping. Even though she was exhausted, fear kept her awake. Which was the worst part of all of this.

Worst of all, Grace hadn't heard from Dot since the gravel incident the day before. She had sat outside on her front porch until dark, but Dot never showed. This meant that either Dot came by while she was still at Molly's office or Dot had been too busy planning her next scheme to show up yet. When you add in the news that Dot lost out on the hotel to Grace, Molly, and Grant, Grace was pretty sure she had every reason to be afraid.

Dinner came and went with no sign of anything untoward, which made it all the more likely that the next bomb to hit would come under cover of darkness. Grace was just about to go upstairs to bed, kitten in tow when the doorbell rang. Her hands shaking just a bit, she cautiously opened the door to find Cole and his dog, Max, standing on the porch.

"Hey," she said, opening the door all the way. "What are you two doing here?"

"We came to keep you company." They walked inside, Cole kissing her on the cheek as he passed her. Max immediately took off to find Ruby, leaving Cole and Grace alone in the foyer. Well, almost alone. "I see the little fur ball has made herself at home," he said, gently petting the kitten on her head.

"She's become my little shadow," Grace said with a laugh. "Now, seriously, what are you doing here? Not that I'm not happy to see you."

"I'm worried about you," he said, the smile gone from his handsome face. "You can't go on like this, Grace. It's not good for your health."

"Try telling that to Dot," Grace said bitterly. "It's not like I'm choosing to live like this. That woman is literally giving me no choice."

"We can deal with whatever happens; what we can't deal with is something happening to you." He pulled her into his arms and held her, resting his chin on her head.

The warmth of his arms loosened the tension in her body, causing her to sigh into his chest. "I wouldn't mind the company if you want to stay," she said, her words muffled.

"Yes, I want to stay, but you're going to sleep. If it's important to you that someone stays up, I'll take my turn."

Grace pulled back to look at him. "First of all, you don't get a turn. You need your sleep way more than I do. Second, this is not your battle to fight, Cole."

"I disagree. Anything that concerns you concerns me. We're supposed to be a team, Grace. Haven't you figured that out yet? Or did you think I spent all that time helping you clean up for fun?"

"Fine, but one of us spends their days operating heavy equipment while the other spends their day decorating and caring for her Granny. I am not willing to risk your health and safety for any reason, especially one like this."

"Okay, it's agreed. Neither one of us is willing to risk the other one. This means that we are both going to sleep and will deal with whatever happens together. In the morning. Like normal people."

Knowing she'd been beaten, she nodded and led him up the stairs. Thankfully, she had a cute pair of pajamas to wear that she quickly changed into before hopping into bed and pulling the covers up to her chin. This was not the first time she had spent the night with Cole, but it was the first time they had slept in a bed together. Even though, technically, there was no difference between a bed and the couch, the bed felt so much more intimate. Especially since it was her bed.

When he returned from the bathroom and saw her bundled up like that, he burst out laughing. "You remind me of the wolf dressed as a granny from Little Red Riding Hood," he said.

"My, what big eyes you have," said Grace.

Cole pulled back the blankets on his side of the bed and laid down, pulling her close to him. "I'm pretty sure that's my line," he said into her hair.

She reached up and kissed him, more thankful than he'd ever know that he was there with her. He allowed the kiss for a couple of minutes before pulling back and snuggling close to her. "You need sleep, darlin'," he said gruffly.

"I need you," she replied shyly.

"And you have me, always," he said, kissing her head. "Sleep, baby girl. I'll be here when you wake up."

Grace was sure she wouldn't be able to sleep, but to her surprise, she drifted off as soon as her head hit his chest. Something about being in his arms made her feel relaxed and safe. At some point, she had no idea how much time had passed; she felt the bed move as Cole jumped out, startling her awake. "What's going on?" she asked sleepily.

"I'm not sure; stay here; I'll be right back."

Unsure if she was awake or having some kind of a nightmare, she laid there for a few minutes listening for sounds of a commotion outside. Then, just as she was about to get up and check on Cole, he appeared, slipping back into bed beside her. "What happened?" she asked.

"I woke up to the sound of my phone alerting me to an intruder outside. I checked the cameras but couldn't see anyone, so I assumed it was an animal. However, I got another alert a few minutes later, so I decided I had better go check it out."

"Did you find anything?"

"I guess not."

"You guess not? That's not very reassuring."

"I didn't see anyone, but it was dark and hard to tell. There are a lot of shadows out there and, therefore, a lot of places to hide. Nice driveway, by the way. When did you put that in?"

Grace told him the story, and they had a good laugh imagining Dot's reaction to finding out she had paid for a place for Grace's guests to park, thereby upgrading the very place she was trying to shut down. Then, since they still had a couple of hours before they needed to get up to do chores, they did their best to wind back down and get some much-needed shut-eye. Tomorrow would take care of itself.

-Days till Easter-

Eleven

Despite going to bed fairly early the night before, Grace and Cole overslept by about an hour, the sun now streaming through the usually dark curtains. They dressed in a hurry, then rushed downstairs and out the door only to stop dead in their tracks at the sight of a large sheet draped across the front of the porch. Cole cautiously lifted the sheet so they could walk under it and down the stairs without running into it.

Before she turned around to look, Grace tried to take a calming breath, but that went out the window the second she saw Cole's reaction. Much like Molly, Cole was not a person quick to anger. In fact, while she had seen him upset, she had never seen him angry. Until now. His hands were clenched, and he looked like he wanted to punch something.

Gathering her courage, she turned around, the sight of the giant sheet, which from a distance looked more like a billboard, causing her to gasp in shock. Written in bold, red letters were the words: Grace's Whorehouse, Two Dollars an Hour. In each corner was a picture of a lantern shining a bright red light. It was humiliating and by far the worst thing Dot had done to her.

As they stood there staring, a couple of cars passed by on the street behind them, honking and waving as if they were in on the joke. This, in turn, only infuriated Cole more. When an old truck pulled up to the curb and stopped, she grabbed his arm, just in case.

Ray, Dot's husband, got out of the truck and approached them, pain written across his face. "I'm so sorry, Grace," he said apologetically. "I had no idea she'd done this. If I did, I swear I would have stopped her."

"Grace lives alone with her elderly grandmother. Do you have any idea what could have happened to her if the wrong person saw this sign," Cole spat out between clenched teeth. "Dot has gone too far, and if you want to help, please go to the police and tell them what you know."

"She's my wife," Ray said softly.

"And Grace will one day be mine." Cole stepped forward until he was mere inches from Ray's face. "I will not let your wife, or anyone else for that matter, hurt her."

"Please, Cole. I know you're upset; you have every right to be. I came here to try to remove that sign before anyone saw it. I beg you, don't ask me to do any more than that."

"I used to have a lot of respect for you, old man, not anymore," Cole said sadly. He turned his back on Ray and spoke to Grace. "Please call the police and take some pictures with your phone. I'm going to go get the ladder out of the garage." He'd only walked a couple of feet before he turned back around. "You know, as much as I love Grace if she ever pulled something like this, it would be over between us. I could never just stand by and watch someone, even someone I loved, harm another person the way Dot has harmed Grace. It ain't right. I know that, and somewhere inside, you know that too." This time, when he walked away, he kept going until he reached the garage and disappeared from sight.

"I guess I had that coming," Ray said sadly. "I really am sorry," he said to Grace. "I've tried talking to her multiple times, but she just tells me to stay out of it. Says I don't have the stones to do what it takes to get the job done. And if this is what it takes, she's right."

"Do you even share her point of view?" Grace asked, curious as to how he felt about everything.

"No," he said with a shrug. "I think what you've been doing has been good for the town. But I've had the benefit of talking to Junior and Bea about it, so I reckon I better understand what y'all are trying to do."

"Why hasn't Dot been talking to them as well?"

"Bea and Dot had a falling out a couple of decades back. Haven't spoken since. So Dot hasn't been a part of any of our conversations."

That made sense to Grace. Ever since this had all started, she'd had a hard time imagining a friendship between Dot and her incredibly kind and loving friend Bea. Someday, she would have to ask Bea about the falling out. It would likely be a story for the ages.

Winterwood was apparently working with a one-man cop shop because Officer Smith was first on the scene, despite the early morning hour. When he stepped out of his car and saw the sign, he let out a low whistle. "That is some nasty work," he said.

Cole returned carrying the ladder. "Good, you're here. Do we finally have enough to arrest Dot? I expect you to take this seriously now that Grace's life has been put in danger."

"Relax, man, I've taken this seriously from the beginning. But I wouldn't exactly consider a sign dangerous. Crass, yes, but not dangerous."

Cole started to speak but closed his mouth and shook his head, muttering about incompetent people as he set up the ladder. Once he got up to the roof, he cursed long and loud words Grace had never heard before. "She attached the sheet with some kind of cement caulk. There is no way I can take this down without damaging the roof."

Officer Smith climbed the ladder Cole had vacated when he climbed onto the roof. He took a good look at the bonding agent and snapped some pictures. "We can make a case for trespassing and harassment, but you might have better luck in civil court over all this property damage. I know you want to see whoever's doing this in jail, but jail's not gonna pay for all this damage."

"I'll pay for it," Ray said from his position on the ground. "There's a local handyman that's pretty good. He might be able to take care of you today. Or you could call a roofing company. Up to you."

"Is there something you'd like to tell me?" asked Officer Smith.

Ray hesitated momentarily, then shook his head, studiously avoiding Cole's penetrating gaze and Grace's pleading one. "Call me when you get someone out here, and I'll come over."

Grace watched him slowly walk back to his truck, his shoulders slumped, shame written on his face. There went a beaten-down man, and Grace felt worse for him than she did herself. A woman like Dot was probably no picnic to live with, and Grace suspected she treated Ray just as badly as she was treating Grace. How she had acquired such a loyal group of followers was anyone's guess.

"Grace?" Cole called out. "If you get me a pair of garden sheers, I'll try to cut this sheet down."

There was a pair in the garage, so she jogged over to find them. Another day with another late start. Dot was costing Cole just as much as she was costing Grace. More actually, since Grace technically only had a job once the first guest showed up. Something had to give before Dot ruined everything.

***

The local handyman showed up after lunch without Grace having called him. That could only mean one thing, Ray had taken care of it like he claimed he would. If only his guilty conscience would guide him to end his wife's reign of terror. Although, if she were honest, she could understand where he came from. It wouldn't be any easier for her to turn Cole in than it was Ray and Grace didn't' have decades of marriage behind her. It was one thing to be disappointed in your spouse's behavior, quite another, to help put them in jail.

The handyman, who had introduced himself as Jim, had surprised her by assessing not only the problem on the roof but any damage that might have been done to the porch when Dot and crew egged it. In addition, he complimented her on her painting skills, which created a lot of goodwill in Grace's eyes.

A couple of hours later, her roof was repaired, and all evidence of Dot's latest and greatest had been removed. It was almost as if it had been a dream. Well, nightmare, really.

Grace had planned to go down to the hotel to take some measurements with Molly, but Dot and her fellow agitators had changed focus and were now busy protesting in front of it. They could have gone anyway, but confronting that mob held little appeal, so they decided to put it off for another day. They still had thirty days until the deal closed, and the hotel was officially theirs anyway, so there was plenty of time. Or, there would be if they weren't coming up against a giant obstacle named Dot at every turn.

For the second day in a row, the doorbell rang after dinner, and for the second time, Grace was cautious about answering it. There was no way to know how many people had seen that horrid banner, and the thought that one of them could show up at her house looking for services was never far from her mind. Thankfully, also, for the second time, it was Cole and Max.

Cole still seemed agitated, his demeanor stiff and straightforward, any hint of affection gone. He walked past her into the house without kissing her, something he hadn't done since they started dating. Concerned, Grace followed him into the dining room. Was he here to break up with her? Were the events of this morning enough to push him over the edge? Grace wouldn't blame him if the answer was yes, but she wasn't sure she could survive without him.

Anxiety started to rise as he pulled out a chair for her and then walked around to the other side of the table where he sat. That was also something he had never done, always preferring to sit side by side, even in restaurants. Yes, they were those people. The ones who couldn't bear to have even the width of a table between them. In their defense, their time together was limited, usually squeezed between work obligations, so they had to make do with what they had.

Cole motioned for her to sit, and reluctantly she obeyed. It was very tempting to run away. He couldn't break up with her if she wasn't there to break up with. In reality, he would follow her if she tried, and she was unlikely to outrun him. Still, maybe she should try. The panic she felt rose in her chest, and her hands started to shake. She couldn't do this.

She stood up so fast her chair fell over and clattered against the hardwood floor as she bolted from the room. She was so focused on the goal at hand she didn't even notice he had followed. But, of course, he did. She made it as far as the stairs in the foyer before he grabbed her and pulled her into his arms.

"Grace, what the heck?" he said, completely bewildered by her admittedly irrational behavior. "Why are you running away from me."

"S-so you c-can't b-break up w-with m-me," she stammered.

"What?" He sat down with his back against the front door, pulling her down and settling her on his lap. "Why would you think I'm breaking up with you?"

"You've never been this formal before," she choked out between gulps of air.

"Breathe, Grace." He held her tightly with one arm while gently rubbing her back with the other. When she could finally breathe normally again, he positioned her to where he could see her face. "I'm sorry if I did something to make you feel this way, but I'm not breaking up with you."

"Then why are you here?"

"Because I'm incredibly concerned about you. I don't want to come off heavy-handed, but I don't think you're safe right now, so I have a few options I wanted to discuss with you.

"Options? What kind of options?" She wasn't sure if it was the lingering effects of her panic attack or something else, but she was having trouble following him.

"Number one, you and Granny move out to the ranch with me. Number two, you and Granny move next door with Gladys, or number three, max and I move in with you." He held up a finger as he counted.

"I don't see how any of those could work," Grace said slowly. When he raised his brow in question, she continued. "My first guest will arrive in a couple of days which rules out options one and two. And while I would love nothing more than for you and Max to move in here, being away from the ranch would make things difficult for you," Grace said with a sigh. "Dot has already cost you so much time; I can't keep asking you to upend your life for me."

"You're not asking; I'm volunteering. Besides, I only need to be here at night, which is not that big of a deal."

"Are you sure?" she asked.

Cole responded by kissing her deeply. "That's so you have no doubt about how I feel about you." He kissed her again. "And that is so you have no doubt I want to be here with you."

"In that case, where's your suitcase?" Before he could answer, three sets of paws came around the corner, led by the rambunctious Piper. She leaped into Grace's lap just as the two dogs climbed on top, licking their faces enthusiastically.

Their arms flailed as they tried to get the situation under control, made all the more difficult by their hysterical laughter. By the time they managed to get back on their feet, Granny had shuffled over to see what all the commotion was about. "You look like quite the family over there," she said, a big grin on her face.

Cole hugged Grace close to his side. "I feel like quite the family."

Grace stood on her tip-toes and kissed his cheek. No matter what happened in her life, moments like these made it all worth it.

-Days till Easter-

Ten

They woke up to...nothing. No strange shadows were lurking near the trees, no eggs covering the porch, and no banners hanging from the roof. In fact, the morning had a feeling of peace to it. Was this the calm before the storm, or had Ray managed to get through to Dot? Knowing Dot, it wouldn't be long before they found out.

After two nights of falling asleep in Cole's arms, she started feeling spoiled. It would be tough when she no longer had a reason for him to stay and he went back to sleeping at his own house. So while she wanted things with Dot to end, suddenly, she wasn't in such a hurry.

Molly came by at lunch to discuss the latest plans for the Easter event. Grace still had not attended a planning meeting, so she needed to catch up on all the details. "The guests will arrive the Friday night before Easter. We will offer a buffet dinner and a bonfire afterward where they can roast marshmallows and make smores."

"That sounds good; what about Saturday? Are we still on for the event in the park?"

"Yes, we'll start with a pancake breakfast, then move to the park for egg dyeing, face painting, and carnival games. There'll be food vendors and the big Easter egg hunt. Then there's the Passion Play at Mayor Allen's Church on Sunday morning."

"Are they still having a potluck dinner afterward?"

"Yes, I signed us up to bring a couple of side dishes and a few dozen tarts."

Grace nodded along as Molly ran down the list. So far, she hadn't said anything that Grace wasn't already expected. "We should do another egg hunt later that afternoon, only, instead of eggs full of candy, we can offer toys and other prizes."

Molly smiled. "I'm sure the kids will love that. Plus, it will keep them busy while simultaneously wearing them out. Which I'm sure the parents will love!"

"I do aim to please. Do we need to have anything planned for Monday? Or will they be leaving?"

"Breakfast should be enough. I have a feeling most of them will want to head home pretty early since they'll have work and school the next day."

"What about Dot? I can see a lot of opportunities for her to try to sabotage us."

"Honestly, I don't know what to do about her. The event in the park is open to the public, and since she still hasn't been caught, we have no reason to ban her."

"Maybe she'll finally do something in front of enough witnesses to get caught."

"Maybe, but how much damage will she do in the process? We must keep her as far away from our guests as possible." Molly looked down at the kitten sleeping peacefully in her lap. "It's too bad; if Dot wasn't such a horrible person, I would have bought one from her."

"We could always go steal one...." Grace said with a shrug. "It's not like she doesn't owe us."

"I can just see us sneaking around her farm in the middle of the night, our faces covered in ski masks as we try to track down her stash of kittens!"

"With our luck, she'll hear us and come out shootin'!" They laughed at the image. "Maybe we should do something to sabotage her," Grace said thoughtfully. "She might start to see things differently if we gave her a taste of her own medicine."

"Might be worth a shot," said Molly. "We could introduce some kind of pest to her corn. See how she likes it when someone decides to ruin her livelihood."

"Yeah, we could slash her tires and leave her stranded out there. At least then, she'd be unable to come to town to harass us."

"We'd have to slash the tires of her stooges, too, though," Molly replied.

"True." Grace thought about it for a minute. "I don't know, it's fun dreaming up ways to get even, but I'm not sure I want to stoop to her level. I feel like I've already been forced to change in ways I don't like."

"In what way?"

Grace shrugged. "I've become a lot more confrontational. As well as a whole lot more paranoid. I'm scared to open my door. Scared to leave my house. Heck, I'm terrified to run my business. Even now, I'm joking about robbing a woman and slashing her tires. The Grace from a couple of weeks ago wasn't like this."

"The scared part sucks, but I'm not sure the confrontational part is bad. I, for one, think it's good that you've gotten more comfortable standing up for yourself. As far as the jokes go, after what you've been through, I doubt anyone would judge you for them."

"Yeah, you're right. Any more news on the hotel?"

"Nope, it's a hurry up and wait game from here on out. The bank approved the loan, but we still have to wait thirty days to close. Plus, there's some kind of historical preservation clause we're dealing with."

"I don't recall hearing anything about that. Should I be concerned?"

"The owners just want to ensure we focus more on restoration than renovation. We're willing to agree to that, but we need to make sure that the contract's wording doesn't box us in, just in case we find significant damage and restoration becomes financially unviable."

"I feel like you're speaking my fears out loud right now," Grace said drily.

"Yes, I know how you feel. I, too, have some reservations. But you must admit, the second we walked inside, it just felt...I don't know, right."

Grace didn't want to admit it, but Molly was right. She had felt something when they were in there. If you couple that with the fact that they beat out the other buyers, it seemed like it was meant to be. Which was all that she could hope for at this point.

***

Later that afternoon, after Molly had returned to her office, Grace set about decorating the outside. She wasn't feeling brave enough to tackle the front porch yet; she would likely leave that until Saturday morning, just in case. But that still left the backyard. Now that it was warm enough to spend some time outside, she wanted to set up a couple of sitting areas for guests to relax, as well as the fire pit area for the bonfire.

The home store she had gone to the other day had an adorable pergola on sale that was made of lightweight metal. Deciding it would be perfect for the fire pit, she spent the next couple of hours assembling it and stringing lights along the top. She placed outdoor couches and chairs around the perimeter, added colorful throw pillows, and then stepped back to admire her work. In her opinion, the empty space had been transformed into a welcoming oasis. She just hoped her guest shared that opinion.

Now that was done, she turned her attention to the deck. It needed a quick power washing to remove all the winter crud, so she fired up her electric power washer and got to work. When she was halfway done, she glanced up and saw Dot's reflection in the sliding glass door. Startled, she screamed and dropped the wand, water spraying everywhere, including at her.

Once the power washer was under control again, she turned it off and turned to face her nemesis. "What are you doing here?" she asked icily.

"I've come to make a deal."

"Oh?" Grace said as she raised her brow. "Why does this feel like a deal with the devil?"

"Because I imagine it is. For both of us."

Grace rolled her eyes. "You wish. You're the only one here with that claim to fame."

"Guess it depends on your perspective."

"Guess so. Now, what do you want?"

"If you agree to back out on the hotel deal, I'll let you keep your business."

Grace shook her head as if to clear it. The words she had just heard were so ridiculous she almost pinched herself to see if she was dreaming again. "First of all, I didn't buy the hotel, so I don't get to make that decision. Second of all, you have no say in my business."

"You know darn well it's just a matter of time before I ruin you, you little brat. If you think the things I've done so far are bad, you have no idea what's in store for you. Do the right thing, and I'll back off. Don't, and you'll have only yourself to blame." She turned around and stomped off the deck. When she was almost to the side of the house, she stopped and turned back to face Grace again. "You have until tomorrow night to make your decision. After that, all bets are off."

If she had been more prepared, she could have recorded that conversation. But who thinks to prepare for confrontations with lunatics? Sure, they obviously happen, but never in her wildest dreams had she expected it to happen to her.

Five, maybe ten minutes passed before Grace dared to walk around to the front of her house. She wanted to ensure that Dot had plenty of time to get back to her car and leave before she went around looking for damages. Since Dot had agreed to a cease-fire, she was hopeful that there wouldn't be any, but at this point, she wasn't taking any chances.

The house appeared to be in its normal state, so Grace took that as a sign that Dot was indeed serious and took off for Molly's office to discuss her terms. After she filled Molly, Grant, and Emilio in on her conversation with Dot, she sat back and waited for their response.

"I'm going to take a page out of our government's playbook and say that we do not negotiate with terrorists," said Grant, clearly agitated by this latest turn of events.

"I would like to point out that our government always says that right before they do, in fact, negotiate with the terrorists," Grace pointed out. "How many prisoner exchanges have we done over the decades? And those are just the ones we know about."

"Okay, fine, but I stand behind the sentiment." Grant paced back and forth. "If we agree to her ridiculous demands, who's to say she'll hold up her end. And how would we even enforce something like that anyway? Regardless of what we do, this woman will be nothing but trouble. I'm not losing out on a solid investment opportunity because of a bully."

"I agree with Grant," said Emilio. "Dot has made her stance perfectly clear on multiple occasions regarding your B&B. She's even gone so far as to harass and torment you on a near-daily basis. There is no reason to trust her claims that she'll leave you alone if you give up the hotel."

"She is a pretty smart woman," Molly chimed in. "Since her previous tactics haven't worked out like she hoped, she's trying something new."

"None of y'all are the least bit concerned about her threat to up her game if we don't comply?" asked Grace. "As the one who's been doing all the suffering, I'm not at all interested in seeing what she deems worse than that lurid banner she hung above my porch."

Grant stopped pacing and leaned his forearms on a chair opposite Grace. "I know this has been the hardest on you, but please don't give up. Eventually, Dot will make a mistake, and we'll be able to end this once and for all."

"And if she destroys my business in the process? What then?"

Grant sighed and ran a hand through his hair. "You're giving her way too much power. You two," he said, pointing to Grace and Molly, "Should be using this to your advantage. People eat up these kinds of stories. You should be videotaping these incidents and posting them all over social media. Get out in front of this and get the people on your side."

That sounds great in theory, and I imagine we'd get a lot of support, but what kind of person will want to vacation at a place that could be turned into a literal trash dump overnight? People go on vacations to relax, not to get involved in neighborly feuds," said Grace.

"Maybe, maybe not. All I'm saying is that we aren't completely helpless here."

Grace looked at Molly, who shrugged. "Okay then, I will do my best to prepare for the next battle wave. Just remember, what she's doing will not stop at the B&B; she will also come for the hotel." That said, Grace got up and left the office. Her life had never felt as out of control as it did at that moment. Maybe she should just take Cole up on his offer to move out to the ranch and call it a day.

-Days till Easter-

Nine

Evie came by that morning after breakfast. She was between customers at the hair salon, The Straight Edge, so she had time to chat about their upcoming get-together the next night. In full-on hostess mode, Grace took her to the new seating area outback, where she served lemonade and freshly baked chocolate chip cookies. It was such a beautiful day, and she felt like she needed to enjoy it while she could. Dot's cease-fire ended in eight hours, and yes, Grace was counting.

"I love what you've done with the place," Evie said as she looked around the backyard.

"You'll have to come back when the flowers are in bloom. The gardening club did a fantastic job. I'm excited to see the results of all their hard work."

"Yeah, I'm not sure what kind of jobs there are for gardeners, but some of those kids have real talent. It'd be a shame if it goes to waste." Evie sipped her lemonade. "So, back to the reason that I'm here. What time works for you tomorrow night?"

"We're thinking six o'clock. If you guys don't mind coming here, we can barbecue some steaks and hang out by the fire pit. Would that work?"

"Sounds good to me. Can I bring anything?"

"Just yourselves. Molly and Grant have opted for a quiet night at home, so it should just be the six of us."

"Six of us? I was only expecting four. Who are the other two?"

"Well, there's you and Jake, Cassie and Conor, and me and Cole."

"Oh, Cassie isn't planning to come. She said she didn't want to be the fifth wheel."

"That's not ideal," Grace said, somewhat concerned. "Can you get her to change her mind? I have a guest checking in tomorrow, and I don't want him to feel like a fifth wheel."

"This isn't some kind of set-up, is it? I'm not sure Cassie will go for that."

"Not at all; I don't even know the guy. I just thought it would be nice to include him, and if we play games, it will be easier to have an even number of people."

"Okay, I can see that. I'll talk to Cassie and let her know her presence has been requested."

"Thank you, so, how have things been going for you?"

"Pretty good. Jake and I have been dating for about nine months now. We've talked about moving in together, but since he lives and works up in the city, and I live and work here, we've been having a hard time figuring out how that would work."

Grace nodded her head in understanding. "Another couple I know had the same problem, so they compromised and moved to Hope Springs. You'll go from a five-minute commute to a thirty-minute one, but it might be worth it."

"Has it worked out for them?"

"As far as I know, yes. I could invite them to our little gathering tomorrow night if you want to meet them?"

"Yeah, please do. There aren't many people our age around here, so it would be nice to meet some new people, maybe make some new friends."

Grace pulled out her phone and shot a quick to Emilio, who replied back a couple of minutes later. "Looks like they're coming," Grace said after she read his reply. She smiled at Evie. "This is turning out to be quite the party!"

Evie laughed. "We should have done this ages ago." She put her glass down and picked up another cookie. "I know I shouldn't ask, but some rumors are going around...."

Ah, yes, the rumor mill in Winterwood was constantly running. If only it were possible to harness its power, the things they could accomplish. Although, maybe she could harness some of its power. She spent the next twenty minutes telling Evie every gory little detail of what Dot had been doing to them, including their conversations. Since Evie worked at a hair salon, Grace was confident she would take care of the rest and spread the news far and wide. It might not do much, but at the least, it should make Dot a little more hesitant to act in public. Which, now that she thought about it, might be the opposite of what she should be trying to accomplish. Oh well, too late now.

"Wow," Evie exclaimed when Grace had finished her story. "It sounds like Dot has become unhinged."

Grace could not agree more. "I'm afraid she will try something tomorrow when Conor arrives. Since I don't know what she's planning, I have no way to try to combat it."

Evie appeared to think about it for a minute. "I think a few high schoolers started a band a while back. You should ask them to come over and set up in the front yard. You can get some neighbors to come over as well. If enough witnesses are present, Dot will have to cancel whatever she has planned or risk exposure. Either way, it's a win for you."

"You know, that sounds like a great idea. I can make it look like it's a welcome party. Thanks, Evie!"

"No problem, happy to help in any way I can. Especially since you're currently keeping the rumor mill off from me. I feel like I owe you one for that."

That was news to Grace. "What's going on?" she asked curiously. I mean, Evie brought it up, so it's not like she was nosy, right?

Evie let out a dramatic sigh. "Apparently, Greg has knocked up another one of my former bridesmaids, in addition to my sister. Of course, everyone wants to know how I feel about this, even though I washed my hands of the whole lot of them the day Shelley married Greg. Honestly, starring in other people's drama gets so tiring."

There were times when Grace would have given anything to have a sibling but hearing about Evie's struggles with her sister made Grace happy to be an only child. "Are you doing okay, though? I can't imagine it's easy hearing about all that."

"Actually, I am okay. I didn't recognize it at first, but my life started over the day of my failed wedding. My entire life leading up to the moment when Greg jilted me now seems like it belongs to someone else. I'm happier now than I've ever been. But I still don't want to rehash it whenever someone sits in my chair for a trim. I've moved on, and it would be nice if everyone else moved on too. Which is why I'm grateful for your current scandal," Evie said with a grin.

"That makes one of us," Grace said, a hint of bitterness in her voice.

They spent another thirty minutes discussing local news and gossip before Evie had to head back to the salon. It had been nice catching up with her, and Grace was looking forward to their get-together the next night. Maybe it would become a regular thing if everyone had a good time. It would be nice to feel like she was part of a group.

***

Grace had spent the rest of the day feeling like a ticking time bomb was strapped around her neck. She wasn't sure what she had expected to happen at six o'clock, but it came and went without so much as a whimper. Now, that didn't necessarily mean anything; Dot seemed to prefer the cover of darkness when she pulled her stunts, which meant they weren't out of the woods just yet.

Too restless to be cooped up inside, she went to the bar to hang out with Cole. Friday nights were usually busy, the end-of-the-week crowd looking to blow off steam before they started on the chores list they often saved for the weekends. She had planned to help, but when she arrived, she saw Ray plopped down in the corner where she usually sat and decided to join him.

"Thanks for taking care of the handyman," she told him.

He looked over at her as if he were surprised to see her. Or maybe he would have been surprised regardless of who it was. Thanks to his wife, he had become just as much of a pariah as she was, according to the citizens of Winterwood. He looked so sad and lonely Grace's heart went out to him.

In response to her earlier statement, he inclined his head. "Told you I would."

"Ray, I know it's none of my business, but are you sure this is worth it?" When he gave her a confused look, she tried to explain. "You're miserable, your name has been ruined in this town, and I can't imagine things are much better at home."

"A man can't just dump his wife at the first sign of trouble. If he did, he ain't much of a man, is he?"

"If this is truly the first sign of trouble, then maybe what Dot needs is a visit to her doctor. There could be something going on that is causing her to act out like this. If that's the case, you owe it to her to find out. Before it's too late, and she ends up behind bars."

Ray stood up and tossed a couple of bills on the bar. "I might just do that." He tipped his hat and then left the bar, leaving Grace to wonder if she'd gone too far.

"Hey beautiful," said Cole as he approached from the other side of the bar. "Everything okay?"

"I suppose we'll find out. Mind if I help out for a while? I don't feel like being at home right now."

"I'm always grateful for the help."

On the weekend, the bar closed at midnight. She hadn't planned to stay that long, but they got busy, and before she knew it, it was closing time. Cole drove them back to

Grace's, where they made a point to search the property one last time before they turned in for the night. Finding nothing, they went inside and fell into bed, exhausted.

Tomorrow would be a big day.

-Days till Easter-

Eight

Conor had texted earlier that morning that he planned to arrive between the hours of two and three that afternoon, giving Grace enough time to decorate the front porch and organize their impromptu concert. Nothing of note had occurred during the night, which meant that either Dot was planning something for when Conor arrived, or Ray had taken Grace's advice. There were no words to communicate how badly she hoped it was the latter.

The band, consisting of Jason and three of his friends, was set to show up around one, and the neighbors, whom Grace had invited the evening before, would come around one thirty. To make it look like a legit party, they had agreed to barbecue hot dogs and hamburgers and to provide an assortment of accompanying sides and drinks. Everyone was excited, and since this was the second block party they had decided to throw in a week, there was talk of making it a regular thing.

Unfortunately, Dot and her fellow mischief makers arrived at noon. They were each wearing a tee shirt with her picture surrounded by a red circle with a line through it and were each carrying a handmade sign with messages such as 'Save our Town,' 'Death to Capitalism,' and 'Just Say No to Big Business.' Dot was also carrying a bullhorn because, of course, she was.

Grace tried calling the police, but since they were standing on the sidewalk and protesting 'peacefully,' there was nothing they could do. How it was possible they lived in a society where people could disturb an entire neighborhood with impunity was beyond her, but it appeared to be the case. Yes, her home was technically a business, but it was also a home in a residential neighborhood. That should count for something, shouldn't it?

Choosing to ignore them, when the band showed up, they made sure to put their speakers as close to the sidewalk as possible. Grace may not be able to stop the protesters, but turnabout was fair play, so there was nothing they could do to stop Grace either. This was bound to turn into a game of chicken, and she was starting to think she should have sold tickets to what would invariably turn into a battle of wills.

The concert started in earnest at one thirty, the music, as Grace had hoped, completely drowning out the protester's chants of 'Save Winterwood.' Finally, a little after two, Conor arrived, but instead of seeming happy to be there, he looked upset to see all the people dancing and having fun. He immediately bolted for his room, and when fifteen minutes had passed, and he still hadn't come back down, Grace went up to check on him.

After lightly rapping on his slightly ajar door, she stepped inside when she saw him sitting in a chair by the fireplace. "Is everything okay?" she asked hesitantly.

"No, it isn't," he said, turning to stare at her. "I told you guys who I was so you could help me protect my anonymity, not so you could invite the whole town out to parade me around like some kind of show dog."

Grace held up her hands. "Okay, wow, that is not what is happening here. No one out there knows who you are, I swear."

"Then what's with all the hoopla?" he asked suspiciously.

The moment of truth had arrived. Did she tell him the truth and risk him wanting to leave, or did she try to hide the truth and risk him finding out later and wanting to leave? Better to be honest upfront. "I don't know if you noticed, but there was a group of elderly people holding signs on the sidewalk." She watched his face for a sign of recognition.

"I think I must have walked by too fast to notice," he said.

"Well, that group is a group of protesters. We knew they were planning to show up today, so we planned this little concert to cover it up."

Conor looked amused. "You planned a concert to drown out the noise of their protesting? And thought that what, I would somehow fail to notice a group of people carrying signs and trying to shout above the music?"

"I admit that it was not a perfect plan. But my neighbors planned to dance as close to the protesters as possible, and we turned the music up as loud as we dared. My hope was that you would think we were quirky or something."

"That is one of the funniest things I have heard in a long time. Should I be concerned that you have protesters? Are you committing unspeakable acts of terror or something?"

"Only if you consider renting rooms to strangers so that my granny and I don't starve an act of terror." The smile on Conor's face was replaced by one of concern, so Grace quickly filled him in on everything that had happened. He was so kinder and more understanding than Grace could have hoped.

"Honestly, someone needs to turn this into a movie," he said when she was done. "People love this kind of heartwarming, David versus Goliath stuff."

"I think I'll leave the movie thing to you," Grace replied dryly. "Right now, I'm just trying to survive."

Conor nodded his head in understanding. "I'm sorry I accused you of being unethical. I hope you can try to understand how it looked from my perspective. Even though admittedly, my perspective was completely arrogant and self-absorbed."

Grace laughed. "I'm sure I would have reacted similarly if I were in your position. Now, you are, of course, free to stay up here, or we would love to have you join us downstairs. Also, I have a small group of friends coming by later for dinner, and we would love for you to join us then, too. Of course, none of them know who you are," she added, in case he got the wrong idea again.

"You know what, I think I'll come check things out. I'm curious to see these guys in action."

"I doubt you'll be disappointed."

***

Dot and her fellow chums had given up around three, which, Grace had to hand it to them, was much longer than she had expected. Especially when you considered they had spent two of those hours next to a loudspeaker and a drum kit. You could call Dot a lot of things, and boy had she, but uncommitted wasn't one of them.

The neighbors left an hour later after taking up a collection for the band, who were elated at simply having the opportunity to play for a live group. Well, that and the copious amounts of hamburgers and hot dogs they had been given. Who knew teenage boys could eat that much?

After that party, Conor had gone to his room to rest while Grace had gone to the kitchen to prepare for the next party. There was a new dessert she wanted to try out in addition to all the sides she needed to make to go with the steaks Cole was planning to grill. Two hours was not enough time, but if she hurried, she could make it.

Cole arrived around five thirty to fire up the grill and help out where he could. He had Max with him, and the two dogs and kitten had a blast chasing each other around the house while their 'parents' worked. Despite the short time she and Cole had been together, at this moment, it really felt like they were a family. And while the logical part of her knew it was too soon, the emotional part wished it were true. She honestly could not imagine her life without Cole.

At a quarter to six, Conor came down and offered to help, so Grace sent him outside to hang out with Cole, who was back to manning the barbecue. And at six o'clock on the Dot, the rest of the guests arrived. After she finished power washing the deck the other day, she added a large table and chairs, where she currently directed everyone to go. In addition to the table and chairs, she had also set up a smaller table with enough space to set up a buffet.

It was a beautiful Spring night, the air warm and crisp, the mosquitoes still dormant. As they sat around the table, talk naturally turned to the upcoming holiday weekend. "Is everyone ready for Easter," Grace asked as she passed around the basket of homemade dinner rolls.

Cassie and Evie gave each other look. "No," Cassie said with a groan. "We volunteered to be in the Passion of the Christ play this year but can't find a Jesus. If someone doesn't volunteer soon, we might have to cancel the play."

"Oh no," Grace said, concern in her voice. "That play has been a tradition for decades. It would be horrible if you had to cancel it."

"That's what we were thinking," Cassie replied. "Anyone here want to volunteer?" She looked around the table at each of the men present.

"Don't look at me," Cole said apologetically. "With everything going on in my life, I truly do not have time."

"I'm afraid I'm out too," said Jake. "I would love to help you out, but since I work up in the city, my schedule would not allow me to make the rehearsals. And I would definitely need rehearsals."

All eyes turned to Emilio, who was studiously looking at his plate. Finally, after a couple of minutes of silence, he spoke. "I know you're all looking at me," he said shyly. "But I can't do it either. I have terrible stage fright and zero acting experience. There's a reason I went into finance...."

"That leaves you," Cassie said, turning her attention to Conor. "We don't usually try to guilt trip visitors, but would you be willing to help us out?

"Um," Grace hurried to intervene. The last thing she needed was for Conor to once again think that she had set him up.

"It's okay, Grace," he said. "I wouldn't mind helping out. Especially since it's for a good cause."

Surprised, Grace looked at Conor, who was staring at Cassie, mesmerized by the brunette's beauty. Not that she blamed him; as long as she had known Cassie, people had reacted to her that way. From the looks of it, she was enjoying the attention.

"Our whole Church thanks you," replied Cassie, her entire face lit up in a smile. "Practice begins tomorrow at two; I'm sure Grace can give you directions."

"Of course," said Grace.

Conversation changed to topics of work and hobbies, namely fishing, since the weather was getting warmer. After dinner, they moved to the fire pit as the night brought cooler temperatures. Grace brought out board games and ingredients to make smores, and they spent the rest of the evening laughing and having a good time.

When the evening was over and everyone had left, Grace snuggled up to Cole in bed. "That was fun," she told him, tracing lazy patterns over his chest.

He picked up her hand and kissed it. "Yes, it was. Our first time hosting a party as a couple."

"I guess it was," Grace said after a few minutes. They'd already hosted a couple of events for Valentine's Day together, but this had been different. This had been personal, not business like the other two.

Piper chose that moment to pounce on Cole's chest, causing both of them to laugh at her adorable antics. If Grace could freeze one moment in time, it would be this one.

-Days till Easter-

Seven

That morning, after breakfast, Grace decided to check in with Conor and make sure he didn't regret volunteering for the play the night before. After the way he reacted when he first arrived, she didn't want to take any chances on there being any more misunderstandings. Especially since last night could easily be misconstrued as an effort to take advantage of him on their part. Not that they had, to her knowledge, none of her dinner guests had known who he was, but she didn't want to take any chances that he thought otherwise.

Once the dishes were clean, she headed up the stairs to his room to find him sitting by the fireplace, Piper asleep in his lap, and Ruby dozing by the fire at his feet. "I hope they're not bothering you," she said, indicating the animals.

"Not at all," he replied. "I've always loved animals. Unfortunately, my parents never allowed me to have one as a kid; we were always too busy chasing the Hollywood dream to have time for a pet."

Grace couldn't help but notice the haunted look in his eyes. Here was a man she could relate to. A man who had known loneliness despite being surrounded by large groups of people. "I'm sorry to hear that," she replied. "I was never able to have a pet either, but ours was more of a money issue than a time one."

Conor nodded his head sheepishly. "You must think I'm a real jerk. I got to do what too few people usually do and live my dream, yet here I am complaining like a spoiled little kid."

"Actually, I thought you seemed like someone forced to live someone else's dream."

That gave him pause. After a few moments of silence, he nodded to the chair beside him. "Would you like to sit down?"

Sensing that he needed to talk, she crossed the room and sat beside him. "I'm sorry if I hit a nerve. I didn't mean to upset you."

"It's not your fault," he said softly. "In the beginning, it was one hundred percent my dream. My parents enrolled me in drama camp the summer after kindergarten, and I fell in love with acting. The thought of transforming into someone else fascinated me. So at the end of summer, I begged and pleaded for them to allow me to go to auditions, and after enough time had passed, they finally agreed."

"Is that when you got the part on Return to Skull Island?"

"No, that came a few years later. First came a bunch of commercials. They were okay, but I wanted to act. Yes, commercials require acting, but I wanted the kind of parts I played in summer camp, and pretending to like cereal wasn't cutting it. But, once my parents saw how much money I could make, they refused to turn them down, regardless of how miserable I was or how inane the commercial."

Grace's heart ached for the little boy. It must have been torture to be so close to his dream yet have it kept just out of reach. "It sounds awful," she said sadly.

He smiled, but it didn't quite reach his eyes. "It's kind of you to think that, Grace. No one else did. My parents kept telling me how grateful I should be that they supported my dream, my old friends were jealous of my new and exciting life, and there was so much competition among the child actors that making friends seemed impossible. So when I finally landed Return to Skull Island, I assumed things would get better. Instead, they got worse."

"How could a TV show be worse than cereal commercials?"

"You never watched the show, did you?"

Grace winced and shook her head, embarrassed to admit that she'd never seen the show that made him famous.

"That explains a lot," he said with a smile. "When I was in summer camp, we were doing Shakespeare and Charles Dickens—"

"As kindergartners?" she interrupted in surprise.

Conor laughed. "The camp was for kids of all ages, kindergarten through high school. But yes, as a kindergartner, I played the lead role in plays like Hamlet and Macbeth. That was the kind of acting role I was interested in. Return to Skull Island was more like a cross between Lost and Legends of the Hidden Temple, only minus the games and for kids."

"That's...hard to imagine," Grace said as she tried to picture that.

"Yeah, I had a hard time, too, and I was the star of the show." He shook his head. "But kids loved it, man. I became so famous I couldn't breathe without being mobbed by a group of fans, kids and adults alike."

"So what happened?" Grace asked gently. When he looked confused, she clarified. "I heard the show got canceled despite its popularity."

Conor nodded his head. "That was me, I'm afraid. I'm ashamed to admit this, but I started acting out. I would refuse to learn my lines, throw tantrums on the set, and became incredibly difficult to work with. My parents tried to get me in line, but I refused. Finally, the brass decided it wasn't worth it anymore, so they canceled the show and went in a different direction while I refused to act again."

"Wow, Conor, I'm so sorry." Grace reached over and gently squeezed his hand.

Conor returned her hand squeeze. "I appreciate that, but I'm pretty certain you didn't come here to hear my sob story."

"Well, in a way, I did. I wanted to check on you and see how you felt about agreeing to act in the Easter play. Now that I've heard your story, I'm more concerned than I already was. I can talk to Cassie and get you out of it?"

"Actually, I'm looking forward to it," he said, surprising them both. "I'm not sure I can ask for a better, meatier role than Jesus!"

"It's certainly better than a cereal commercial," she laughed.

"That it is. I still need to get those directions from you," he said.

"It's literally four blocks down the street. Only Church on the left."

"Only Church?"

"Well, there are three churches all within a block of each other, but the other two are on the right side of the street. Also, there's a parking lot to the left of the Church. It's confusing because it looks like it's part of someone's home, but it's not." Conor looked confused, which made Grace nervous. "How about I drop you off for this first practice? I can pick you up when you're done...unless a certain brunette offers to bring you back...."

Conor smiled in response to her not-so-subtle hints. "What can you tell me about Cassie?" he asked curiously.

"Not much unless you want me to ruin the surprise."

"The surprise?"

"Yeah, the part where you guys get to ask each other a bunch of awkward getting-to-know-you questions."

"Can you at least tell me if she's single," he grinned.

"According to Evie, the answer is yes. That she showed up last night without a date backs that up.

"That's good enough for me. Thanks, Grace."

"Anytime," she said as she stood up to leave. "We'll need to leave after lunch, so you have a couple of hours to yourself. Let me know if you need anything."

"Will do," he said, giving her a two-finger salute.

Grace left his room and went down the hall to her own. Something had bothered her since her conversation with Ray the other night, and she knew just who to see for some answers.

***

After Grace dropped Conor off and got him settled at the Church, she headed over to Junior and Bea's to talk to Bea. When she arrived at their farm, she waved to Junior, who was out in his tractor, tilling the field to prepare it for planting season. Then, she knocked a couple of times on their front door and went inside when she heard Bea call out for her to enter. "In the kitchen," Bea yelled after Grace had closed the door.

She navigated her way through the living areas to the kitchen, where she found Bea baking something that smelled heavenly. "Whatcha making?" asked Grace. She was always looking to expand her culinary skills, especially since she had spent most of her life lacking them.

"I'm trying out a new Easter recipe. These big holidays tend to be my best money makers since most families have get-togethers and what have you. So what's up?" she asked as she looked up from where she was braiding a large section of dough. "Hopefully, you haven't had any more 'surprises.'"

She didn't have to specify what she meant by 'surprises'; they both knew she was referring to Dot. "None today, but she is why I'm here."

"Oh," Bea said as she raised her brow.

"I was talking to Ray the other night, and he told me that this was the first time Dot had acted out like this. So, I suggested he take her to the doctor in case she has something wrong with her."

"That's not a bad idea," Bea shrugged. "But I'm not sure I agree with Ray."

"That's why I'm here. I heard you had a falling out with Dot years ago, so I figured if anyone would know if this was Dot's normal behavior, it would be you."

"Does it matter? Even if something is wrong with her, that doesn't excuse her behavior."

"No, it doesn't. But I'd hate to think that the whole town is shunning her when we should be trying to get her some help."

Bea walked around the counter and gave Grace a hug. "You have a kind heart, sweetie. But to answer your question, while Dot has certainly upped her game as of late, she has always been this way. At least as long as I have known her."

"Why did you have a falling out? If you don't mind me asking?"

Bea sighed. "It was a long time ago. Around six months after I'd first opened the bakery. I, of course, was on cloud nine. I'd wanted to open a bakery for years and was finally doing it. Dot didn't think our town needed a bakery. She felt I was foolish and wasting money on a venture doomed to fail. She became angry when I didn't fail within the first six months, as she had predicted."

"That's terrible," said Grace. "Friends are supposed to build you up, not tear you down."

"That was my thought as well. It all came to a head when she attended a town council meeting and tried to get them to shut down my business. She claimed that she had gotten food poisoning from some of my pastries. The same pastries the council had ordered earlier that day for the meeting that night."

Grace's jaw almost hit the floor. "I can't believe she did that to you. I mean, after everything she has done to me, I can believe it. But...she was supposed to be your friend."

"She was supposed to be your granny's friend too. But, sadly, friendship means nothing to that woman."

"Obviously, she failed since you're still in business. So, what happened?"

"The council refused to eat the pastries they had bought, but the secretary had already tried one. When a couple of days had passed, and she still hadn't gotten sick, the council decided that Dot must have gotten sick from something else she had eaten and denied her request to shutter my business."

"Or she lied about having been sick in the first place."

"That was my thought too. But at the time, I had no way to prove it. I did, however, refuse to speak to her ever again."

"I don't know how to feel right now. I didn't want anything to be wrong with Dot, but at the same time, it would have been nice if there was a reason for her antics; other than she's a horrible person."

"I know, honey. I felt the same way." Bea returned to working with her dough as she got it ready for the proving drawer. Her kitchen was state of the art, even though her farmhouse was almost as old as Grace's.

Grace walked over to Bea and gave her another hug. "Thank you for talking to me. I'm sure it wasn't easy bringing up bad memories like that."

"No, but it lost its sting a long time ago. I just wish you weren't on the receiving end of Dot's repeat performance."

"Me too. Let me know when you're ready to sell some of that amazing bread you're baking. I'll be first in line!"

"You got it, kiddo!"

Now that she'd gotten the answers she had come for, she grabbed her keys and headed back to her car. There was still a lot of work to be done for the day. She had her own cooking to do as well as some extra cleaning now that they had a guest staying with them. But, at least now, she could put her concerns about Dot to rest.

-Days till Easter-

Six

About an hour after breakfast, Grace received a frantic call from Molly asking her to immediately come down to the office. Concerned that something was wrong with the baby, she flew out the door without thought and ran five blocks down the street. When she arrived, she found everyone seated in the conference room. "What's wrong?" she asked as she gasped for breath. "Are you okay?" she asked Molly directly.

Molly's eyes grew big as she realized what had happened. "Oh, Grace, I'm so sorry; I didn't mean to scare you like that. Both the baby and I are fine."

"Well," Grace said, still panting. "That's good to hear."

Grant pulled out a chair for Grace and handed her a bottle of water. "Next time, we'll make sure we're a little more careful about how we word our emergencies," he said, giving his wife a look.

Molly looked back at him with a sheepish grin. "I guess I did overreact just a tad," she said, holding her thumb and forefinger a tiny bit apart for emphasis.

Grace took a drink from the water bottle. Once she had regained her breath, she turned to face everyone. "So what's this about?"

Emilio slid a stack of papers across the table to her. "We just received these this morning."

As far as she could tell, and she was certainly no expert, Emilio had handed her a stack of legal papers. Specifically, ones involving a lawsuit. But neither she nor anyone else was named. Dot, however, appeared to be the plaintiff. "What is this?"

"Dot has decided to sue the hotel owner for discrimination."

"I don't understand. I thought things only happened fast on TV? How could she have hired an attorney, filed a lawsuit, and served the defendant in just a few hours."

"She filed the day she found out her offer wasn't accepted," Emilio shrugged. "It seems she had anticipated the outcome and prepared just in case."

"Okay, but what does this have to do with us?"

"The hotel owners have backed out of the sale, citing this lawsuit," Grant said, pointing to the papers. "Their lawyer believes he can get the case tossed out, but they don't want to take any chances."

"Will they let us continue with the purchase if they win?" she asked. This was certainly unexpected. Could it be a sign that they had made a mistake?

Grant sighed and shook his head. "I don't know. After everything that's happened as of late, they're considering holding onto it and trying to sell at a later date. They feel responsible for everything Dot and her cabal have been doing, and this lawsuit has only cemented their beliefs."

"That's ridiculous," Grace said, outraged on their behalf. "Dot is responsible for Dot. It is not their fault that she's gone off her rocker."

"On that, I'm sure we all agree. But unless we can change their minds, which is likely impossible, at least until after the lawsuit is resolved, there's nothing we can do."

The room went silent as everyone processed the news. "I guess this means that Dot's offer of a cease-fire last week was nothing more than a ruse," Grace said bitterly. "I guess you were right not to 'negotiate' with her."

"I know it's hard but try not to let it get to you. Everything will work out in the end." Molly reached over and squeezed her hand.

"I want to believe you, I really do. But it appears there are no lengths Dot is unwilling to go to to get what she wants. Besides that, this weekend is the only opportunity she will get to sabotage us for a while, so there is no doubt in my mind that the worst is yet to come." Grace stood up to leave. There was nothing she could do here and too much to do back at the house.

When she reached the door, she turned back for one last question. "Out of curiosity, what type of discrimination is she claiming?"

"Ageism," replied Grant. "According to the paperwork, she submitted an offer well above asking price, yet she was denied in favor of a group of young people."

Grace shook her head. "Do you think she honestly believes she was turned down due to her age? Or is this just another one of her ploys?"

"Hard to say," Grant said with a shrug. "I suppose, at this point, it doesn't matter."

Grace nodded. "I'll see you guys at dinner."

Once outside, she started her trek back up the street at a much slower pace than before. As she passed the town hall/community center/fire department, Mayor Allen popped out and waved her down. She briefly debated pretending she hadn't seen him but decided not to be petty, so she turned right and walked over to him.

"We've missed you at the morning meetings," he said. "I can't help but feel that I'm the reason you've been avoiding them."

"I would like to say that you're wrong, but I would be lying," she replied.

The mayor nodded. "That's what I was afraid of. I never meant to hurt your feelings, Grace. Nor was I taking Dot's side against yours."

"You could have fooled me," she said. "Everyone in town knew that Dot was the one who egged my house. Everyone but you, it seems."

Allen sighed. "I knew it, too; I just didn't want to believe it. It was much easier to stomach a group of kids playing a prank than to think that a grown woman would do something like that."

"Why?" In her mind egging someone's house was rotten regardless of who did it. The damage was not commensurate with the age of the perpetrator.

"Why? Because kids do stupid things without thinking of the consequences. If a group of kids had done it, it would have been because they thought they were being funny. Dot, on the other hand, would have known better. So if it were her, there would have been no mistaking her intent."

"And we didn't," said Grace. "Just like we didn't any of the other times."

They stood there silently for a moment, neither knowing what to say. Dot had been a member of the community for a long time. Other than the incident with Bea decades ago, another incident that couldn't be proven, Dot had always seemed above reproach. Although, maybe that wasn't entirely true. The entire town sure had jumped aboard the Dot-shunning train pretty quickly. That was unlikely to happen if she were indeed a pillar of the community like she claimed to be.

"I'm sorry, Grace," Mayor Allen said, finally breaking the silence. "We're trying to do what we can to solve the problem. At this point, that's all I know to do."

"I appreciate that. Hopefully, we'll succeed sometime before she ruins my business." Mayor Allen winced, and Grace immediately felt terrible. None of this was his fault; his hands were tied just as much as everyone else's. Taking out her frustrations on him was not going to solve anything. "I'm sorry, that was my frustration talking."

"No, you're right. But if we don't put an end to Dot's antics soon, it's going to cost all of us. We have the town lawyers looking into it. I'll let you know if they come up with anything."

"Thanks," said Grace. "I'll try to come to the meeting tomorrow. Between chores and breakfast, it's difficult, but I'll try to make it work."

He extended his hand, and she shook it willingly, her earlier hesitation gone. "I look forward to seeing you."

After the conversation, he went back inside, and she continued her walk home. At least one good thing had come out of her trip.

***

Around eight o'clock that night, Grace got an alert on her phone that motion was detected outside on the porch. She checked the camera and, seeing it was Ray, went downstairs to see what was happening. Since Cole was still down at the bar, she could only hope this was a social visit and not part of some nefarious scheme of Dot's. Although, if it were a social visit, he would have rung the bell...

She opened the door and stepped onto the porch, but there was no Ray. Confused, she walked around to the side of the porch and found him sitting in the dark on her wicker sofa. The darkness made it hard to tell for sure, but he looked like a man defeated. His shoulders were slumped, his head hung so low his chin rested on his chest. "Ray?" she said softly. "Are you okay?"

Several seconds passed before he responded. "I took Dot to the doctor today."

"What happened?" she asked gently. Ray's voice was so sad and depressed Grace automatically assumed the worst.

"What happened is Dot got extremely angry. Accused me of tricking her, which I did to get her there, and then refused to cooperate with the doctor. However, the doc felt he got enough information out of her to declare that she was of sound mind, and not suffering from some kind of mental decline like I had hoped. Well, you know what I mean."

Grace had no idea how to respond to that. After her conversation with Bea the day before, she had expected this outcome. But like Ray, a part of her had still hoped that there was an explanation for Dot's behavior other than she was a close-minded jerk hell-bent on destroying anything and anyone she disagreed with. "I'm sorry, Ray. I hope you're not in too much trouble," she said, wincing as she realized how pathetic her words must sound.

"When we got back home, she tried to kick me out. But the farm is in my name only, and thankfully I was smart enough to get a prenup before we married. When I reminded her of that, she packed a bag and went to stay with a couple of her followers. Grace," he lifted his head and looked her straight in the eye. "I don't think she's coming back."

His voice had so much pain and sorrow that tears welled in her eyes. She couldn't understand why, but he obviously loved his wife very much and was now paying an incredibly steep price for trying to save her. To save them. She moved to sit next to him on the couch and wrapped her arm around his shoulders. "I'm so sorry," she whispered, more than aware of just how inadequate those words were. "Is there anything I can do for you?"

He shook his head. "No, but there's something I can do for you. Tomorrow morning I will go to the police and tell them what I know."

"Oh, Ray, you don't have to do that," she replied, shocked by his words. She had wanted this all along, but now that he was willing, she found she couldn't let him go through with it. Yes, Dot needed to be stopped, but not by him. The price he would pay was just too high.

Ray patted her on the knee. "I should have done it when she egged your house. I didn't want to see it before, but Dot is like a tornado weaving a path of destruction through every step she takes. If I don't stop her now, it's only a matter of time before she crosses a line she can't uncross."

"But if you're the one who stops her, your marriage will be over for good. She'll never forgive you, Ray. I can't ask you to destroy your marriage for me."

"Whatever happens will be on Dot's conscience, not yours. What matters now is my conscience, and I can't continue to sit back and watch her hurt people I care about for no other reason than she can't handle change." He stood up and held out his hand to her. "I didn't come here so you could talk me out of this, though I appreciate you trying. I came here because I thought you should be the first to know."

Grace shook his hand and followed him to the front of the porch. "Thank you, Ray. Please let me know if you need something. We all still care about you."

He tipped his hat to her then disappeared into the darkness, his truck, she assumed, parked on the side of the house. A few minutes later, Cole's truck came screeching to a halt by the curb in front of the house. "Are you okay?" he asked, giving her a once over as he looked for signs of harm. "I got the alert and saw a man on the porch. I almost had a heart attack when I watched you step onto the porch a couple of minutes later."

"I'm fine," she said in a soothing voice as she attempted to reassure him. "The man was Ray, which I knew before I came outside."

Cole looked confused. "What was Ray doing here?"

Grace filled him in on their conversation, the words more painful the second time around. "He's going to ruin his marriage, Cole. And I feel like it's my fault."

Cole put his hands on either side of her face and turned it up to look at him. "Hey," he said gently. "None of this is your fault. Dot is the only one here who deserves any blame. If she chooses to end her marriage, that's on her, okay?"

"I'm the one who told Ray to take Dot to the doctor and kept pushing him to go to the police. If I had minded my own business...."

"Baby, listen to me. You tried to do the right thing at every turn. You are not responsible for the actions of others. Whatever happens to Dot will be a direct result of her actions, not yours. And honestly, Ray is better off without her."

"I thought that too. But you didn't see the heartache in his eyes. He loves her, Cole. And this is killing him."

Cole pulled her into his arms and held her close. "If I were in his shoes, I would feel the same way. But Ray is a grown man. A good man. You need to let him do what he thinks is right."

It was hard to admit, but Cole was right. They always say that the hard thing to do and the right thing to do are often the same. Which is probably why she felt so bad. At least now she wouldn't have to worry about Dot lurking behind every corner. Maybe Molly was right, and everything really would be okay.

-Days till Easter-

Five

Grace was in the kitchen working on some new recipes while chatting with Conor when Cole walked in. Surprised to see him so early in the day, she immediately stopped what she was doing and turned to face him. "What's wrong?" she asked, concern written all over her face.

"Dot got away," he replied glumly.

"Got away? From what?"

"Ray went to the police station this morning just as he said he would. He gave his statement and told them that Dot was staying out at the Kerr Farm with Gene and Betty. When the police knocked on the front door, Dot ran out the back, jumped in Gene's tractor, and took off for the corn fields."

The image of an eighty-year-old woman fleeing the cops in a tractor was too much for Grace to bear, but Cole seemed so serious she did her best to keep a straight face. Until she made the mistake of looking at Conor. One look at his wide-eyed expression was all it took for her to lose her composure and burst out laughing. Soon after, Conor joined in the laughter while Cole stood there staring at both of them with an annoyed expression.

It took a couple of minutes, but Grace eventually pulled herself together. "I'm sorry," she said, wiping the tears from her eyes. "This has obviously upset you very much. What happened next?"

"Is this Dot woman a fugitive on the lam now?" Conor asked. He coughed a couple of times to hide his laughter.

"I'm glad you both find this so funny," Cole growled. "Meanwhile, Dot's latest antics are going to cost me an entire day's worth of work."

Sobered by the anger in his voice, Grace immediately stopped laughing. "I don't understand; what does this have to do with you?"

"After Dot left Gene's, she made her way over to my land and bulldozed her way through several sections of fence, letting a third of my cows out in the process. She then took out a couple of my heated water troughs before finally dumping the tractor in the pond and running off into the woods."

There were no words to describe how Grace felt at that moment. She had helped Cole enough times to understand just how costly and upsetting that damage would be. "If you can give me a couple of minutes to put this stuff away, I can come over and help you repair the damage," she said quietly.

"I can help, too," said Conor. "I don't know much about repairing fences, but I could at least help hold the boards or something."

"I didn't come here to ask for help; I came here to update you on Dot. But I would appreciate the help if you're willing. I'll meet you over there. Gene is supposed to come by this afternoon so we can try to get his tractor out of my pond."

Cole left without another word, which caused Grace more than a little bit of anxiety. She quickly started putting ingredients away while making a mental list of things she needed before they left. "I need to change before we leave," she said to Conor. "The fields are pretty muddy right now, so if you have a pair of boots or something, you might want to change as well." She felt bad for asking, knowing the answer was likely no. Who brought work boots and old clothes on vacation?

"I have an old pair of tennis shoes that will work." Conor was quiet for a minute. "I realize I don't know Cole very well," he said thoughtfully. "But that seemed out of character for him."

Grace nodded her head in agreement. "It's rare to see him angry. But Dot really crossed the line this time. While Cole owns the bar in town, the ranch is his main business. Losing a day's worth of work, not to mention the money it will cost for the replacements, will set him back."

"Seems like a rough business if losing one day will hurt that much."

"It's not just one day," she sighed. "There have been many missed days due to him helping me out when Dot targeted me. The more days he misses, the further behind he gets." She started packing an ice chest with leftovers they could eat for lunch. "But yes, it is a rough business. The hours are long, and the margins are tight." She added plenty of water bottles and threw in some tarts for good measure. "I think I'm ready. I just need to go change."

"You must really love him," he said quietly.

There was something in his tone of voice. "Yes, why?"

"I've never known a woman so quick to volunteer for dirty, manual labor before." He smiled, but it didn't reach his eyes.

"It's nothing he wouldn't do for me."

"You're very fortunate, Grace. Don't ever forget that."

Grace nodded. "I'll be ready in five." She left him in the kitchen as she hurried upstairs, wondering what that was about. There must have been someone in his life who he had loved and lost. Everyone deserved to be with someone who loved them. Hopefully, one day, he will find his person. Who knows, maybe he already had.

***

They pulled onto the road to Cole's about ten minutes later, the mood in the car a mixture of excitement and trepidation. "I've never been to a ranch before," said Conor. "Will there be horses?"

Grace glanced over at him. "Yes, Cole has horses, but at this time, they'll likely be out in a field somewhere. I can always talk to Cole about taking you for a ride sometime if you'd like?"

"It's okay; I wouldn't want to impose."

The sadness was back in his voice, so Grace vowed to remember to talk to Cole later that night. While it was true that Cole was lacking time these days, others could take Conor. She pulled up next to the house and parked beside Cole's truck. "We're here," she said. "And from the looks of it, so are a few others." Several other trucks were parked nearby, one of which looked like it belonged to Gene.

"I've been thinking," said Conor. "I understand why this Dot woman is in trouble, but why aren't the other protesters in trouble as well? Take this Gene fellow. He's just as guilty as Dot, yet somehow he's become a victim."

"That's a good point. I don't know why he's not in trouble. It was hard enough to get the police to go after Dot. I guess they've decided that since she's the ringleader, she should be the one punished."

Conor looked at her thoughtfully. "I don't know," he said with a shrug. "It just doesn't feel right. If Dot's actions are bad enough to justify putting her in prison, then I think they should all go to prison."

"I highly doubt she's going to prison," Grace said as she rolled her eyes. "And honestly, I don't even care if she does. I just want her to stop harassing me."

"I understand that. It just doesn't seem like her crimes are proportionate to the punishment. I mean, the police showed up to arrest her for egging your house. Where I come from, that's considered a harmless prank."

Grace took a deep breath. "You make it sound like we're trying to put someone's innocent granny behind bars. Dot has made repeated calculated efforts to ruin my business, resulting in numerous cases of property damage, expenses, and sleep loss. Not to mention the psychological toll it took on my mental health and the countless hours we spent cleaning up after her 'harmless pranks.'" Grace took another deep breath to tamp down her anger. "Now she has cost Cole thousands of dollars, and don't get me started on how much it will cost Gene to try to repair his tractor. If you honestly believe that poor Dot is 'harmless,' you are more than welcome to take her home with you."

She got out of the car and slammed the door, so angry that tears of frustration filled her eyes and threatened to spill down her cheeks. Thankfully, she was wearing sunglasses which hid the evidence. She'd managed to put quite a bit of distance between her and Conor before she heard his door open and close.

"Grace," he called out. "Please wait."

It was tempting to ignore him and keep going, but not only was he her guest, he was now stranded out here without her. So, she stopped and stood silently while waiting for him to catch up. When he reached her, she started walking again.

"I'm really sorry," he said a few minutes into their walk. "I was out of line. All I saw was a group of old people holding signs the day I arrived. I had no idea how severe or costly things had become for you."

"Dot used to be a friend of my granny's," Grace said softly. "Because of Dot, friendships have ended, and worst of all, her marriage is on the verge of ending. And for what?" Grace stopped walking to look at him. "If anyone wished this was nothing more than some 'harmless prank,' it's me."

"I understand, and I really am sorry. I have no right to stick my nose in your business."

Grace shrugged. "It's definitely not an ideal situation. No one wants to send an eighty-year-woman to jail. Not even me. Gene, on the other hand...." They turned to watch as several men with chains and a tractor tried to drag Gene's tractor out of the pond.

"What do you think will happen to her?"

It took her a couple of minutes to think of a response. What did she think would happen to her? "I imagine she'll end up with some kind of community service. If we decide to sue her, she'll end up paying for damages. And I guess the rest will depend on her and Ray."

They started walking toward the pond. "You really think they'll get divorced?"

"I have no idea. Honestly, Ray would take her back in a heartbeat. So I guess it's really up to Dot."

When they reached the pond, they found Cole, who put them on fence repair duty. Grace had helped him do it enough times that she knew what to do and could work without supervision. Conor had no idea what to do but was happy being the 'muscle.' Between the two of them, they had the fence repaired by mid-afternoon.

It took the rest of the guys slightly longer to pull the tractor out of the pond. The ground was so muddy the tires couldn't get good enough traction. They finally had to grab some boards from the barn and lay them under the tires to keep them from spinning. Once it was finally out of the pond, they were able to tow it out of the field and load it up on a flatbed to take to the repair shop in town. Since it was time for planting season, this delay was really going to cost Gene.

Speaking of Gene, when he saw the damage that had been done to his tractor, he disavowed Dot on the spot. Which was a little too late if you asked her, considering he had to drive past the damage his tractor had done to Cole's property to get to the pond. While a small part of her sympathized with Gene, the larger part felt like he had gotten what was coming to him. Yes, the damage to the tractor outweighed the damage to her house and Cole's, but in her opinion, he was just as responsible as Dot was. Sometimes bad things happen to good people, and sometimes bad things happen to bad people. It was not for her to decide which category Gene was in.

-Days till Easter-

Four

Molly and Grace sat at the dining room table, stuffing plastic Easter eggs full of candy. Somehow, despite their best efforts, they had ended up agreeing to the arduous task. Since they planned on at least one hundred kids showing up, they had decided to stuff fifteen hundred eggs. That was seven hundred and fifty eggs each. They were going to be there awhile.

They had tried to recruit Gladys and Granny, but the two crafty old ladies had claimed to have some mysterious appointment to get to. On the other hand, Piper was happy to help; only her idea of helping was to bat the eggs off the table and then jump down to chase them around the room. More than one had ended up in hard-to-reach places.

"You heard any news about Dot," asked Molly.

Grace looked up from the egg she was stuffing with tootsie rolls and bubble gum. "No, have you?" she asked suspiciously.

Molly shook her head. "No news on Dot and no news on the lawsuit. Although, from what we've heard, the lawyer thinks these new developments will make it easier to get the case dismissed."

"Are the sellers still refusing to sell?"

"As of now, yes. But Grant has been working on them, so we'll see."

She stuffed another egg. "I wish they would find Dot already; it feels like she's even more dangerous now that everyone is looking for her."

"I suppose," Molly said thoughtfully. "It's not like she's a terrorist, though. She's more likely to be hiding than planning something."

"Why can't she do both? I mean, she's got nothing but time."

Molly wrinkled her nose. "Yeah, I guess you're right. It would just be nice if this nightmare was finally over."

"Hey, you're preaching to the choir over there. I would love to believe that we are safe again. But, and this is a big but, I won't feel comfortable letting my guard down until Dot has been found."

As they continued to work, Conor came downstairs and joined them. "Hey ladies," he said as he sat at the table. "What have we here?"

"The most exciting afternoon activity you have ever seen," replied Grace. "Want to join us?" she asked hopefully.

Conor laughed. "I would love to." He picked up an egg and started filling it with candy.

"How's practice going?" asked Molly.

"Pretty good," he replied. "I've managed to memorize my lines, which is a huge relief. It's been so long since I've had to that I was afraid I might have lost my touch."

"Has this reignited your passion for acting?" asked Grace. As soon as those words left her mouth, she wished she could take them back. The last thing she wanted to do was make him feel bad. Thankfully, he seemed unbothered by her intrusive question.

"In a way, I think maybe it has," he answered thoughtfully. "I'm not ready to jump back into Hollywood, but I am considering joining the local theater group when I get home. If you remember," he said to Grace. "Plays were what I originally fell in love with in the first place."

Grace nodded her head. "I remember you telling me that; I just never put it together. When most people think of acting, they tend to think of Hollywood. It never dawned on me there were other avenues to explore."

"He picked up another egg, laughing as Piper tried to swat it out of his hand. "To be honest, until recently, I thought the same way you did. I feel like I owe you a debt of gratitude, Grace. You've given me back my dream."

Too choked up to respond, Grace smiled and squeezed Conor's hand. As if sensing her friend's distress, Molly chimed in. "Maybe we should have named this place the Miracle Inn after all," she joked to lighten the mood.

"That would have been a great name," exclaimed Conor. "I bet this place would be booked year-round if you named it that."

Grace swallowed past the lump in her throat. "Can you imagine how high people's expectations would be if we did that? The demands would be out of this world."

The room went silent as they all imagined the kinds of customers they would get. Some would likely be sad and tragic, but others would be the worst kind of entitled people. The ones who would come with outrageous demands and lawyers on speed dial. No, thank you, thought Grace. There wasn't enough money in the world to put up with that.

They were finally done a few hours later, thanks to Conor's help. If it hadn't been for his extra set of hands, the task would have taken all day. "What's on the agenda for the rest of your day?" Grace asked Conor.

"I'm supposed to meet Cassie for dinner at a local diner before practice tonight."

Grace raised her brow. "As in a date?"

A smile broke out on Conor's face. "A friendly date. She wants me to give her a couple of pointers."

"So you've told her about your acting past?"

"No, but I'm doing a good enough job that people have started to notice. It's the little things, like knowing certain terminologies and how to set up lights to get the best lighting."

"That makes sense. Who is Cassie playing?"

"She plays Mary Magdalene, and Evie plays my mother."

Grace nodded her head. "Interesting," she tried to smile. "Anyway, I hope you have fun tonight. I'm really looking forward to seeing the play on Sunday."

Conor gave her a strange look. "Do you have a problem with me hanging out with Cassie?"

"Not at all," Grace replied in surprise. "I actually think you two would be good for each other. If it wasn't for the fact that you live so far away."

That gave him pause. "Something I need to think about," he said. "I'll see you guys later."

Conor headed for the stairs, and Grace turned to Molly. "I seem to have a habit of sticking my foot in my mouth."

"You didn't say anything that wasn't true."

"No, but it also isn't my business." Her phone dinged, and she pulled it out of her pocket to check her messages. Seeing it was from Cole, she immediately opened it to see what he said. 'Hey babe, be ready by six; wear something nice.'

"What's wrong?" Molly asked after seeing the look on her face.

"Cole sent me a rather vague message telling me to be ready by six."

"Sounds like a date to me," Molly said with a shrug. "Something the two of you are long overdue for."

"You don't mind looking after Granny?"

"Of course not. I've started to get into watching game shows with them. We've got quite the competition going right now."

Grace wasn't sure if she was serious, but she appreciated it all the same. "Thanks, Molly."

"Have fun tonight; you've earned it."

***

Grace was ready and waiting on the porch when Cole arrived at six o'clock on the dot. Since he had asked her to wear something nice, she had put on a cute, blue long-sleeved peasant dress with matching sandals. Her red, curly hair was loose and flowing down her back, and she wore just enough make-up to enhance her features.

When Cole got out of the truck to greet her, her breath caught in her throat. If Cole was handsome when he was working, which he was, he was drop-dead gorgeous when he was dressed up. He wore black jeans, a button-up dress shirt that matched the color of his blue eyes, and a black cowboy hat and boots.

"You look beautiful tonight," he said as he kissed her cheek. "Are you ready to go?"

"You don't look so bad yourself," she drawled. It was the understatement of the century, but judging by his deep chuckle, her drooling over him had not escaped his notice.

He took her hand, led her to the passenger side door of his truck, and then helped her into the cab. Once she was inside, he went to the driver's side and got in. "I know that since I started staying with you at night, we've technically been spending more time together, but for some reason, it feels like we've hardly seen each other at all."

"Yeah, I know how you feel. It's because all we seem to do anymore is work. Besides, even though you've been staying the night, we've been so tired we've been going to sleep as soon as you get here."

"It will be nice when things calm down again. For tonight though, I want it to be just us. No talk of work or Dot or any other problems. Is that okay with you?"

"There's nothing I want more. So where are we going?"

"A buddy of mine told me about this fancy French restaurant in the city. I thought you might like to go there?"

Grace nodded her head thoughtfully. "That does sound nice, but...."

Cole raised his brow. "But?"

"But grabbing a pizza here in town and spending the night at the ranch sounds even nicer. Unless you really have your heart set on the French restaurant," she added hastily.

"There ain't a French restaurant in the world that could hold a candle to spending the night alone with you," he laughed. "I just don't want you to feel like I never take you anywhere nice."

Memories of the time he told her about his ex-wife popped into her head, and she wondered how much of his insecurities still stemmed from that relationship. In a show of love and support, she moved to the middle seat and wrapped her arms around his neck. "I appreciate the thought, I really do. And someday it might be nice to go to the restaurant. But honestly, all I want to do is spend some time alone with you. And I would love to do it at the ranch."

Cole raised his hand to cup her face and looked deeply into her eyes. "You really mean that?"

The intensity of his gaze stole her breath as well as her words, so she nodded instead. Seconds later, his lips were on hers, and the rest of the world faded away. They never did get the pizza, opting instead to go straight home.

Grace would have happily spent the rest of the night at the ranch, but they were still uncomfortable leaving Granny home alone. So they snuck inside the house around midnight and up the stairs to their room. When had it become their room? She didn't know, nor did she care. All that mattered was that they were together, and this time, when they went to bed, they didn't immediately go to sleep.

-Days till Easter-

Three

They woke up a little late that morning and, once again, hurried to get dressed. Luckily the animals couldn't care less about their appearance, so there was no need to dress to impress. When Grace was finished getting ready, she walked over to Cole, wrapped her arms around his waist, and laid her head against his back. "You've only been staying here for about a week, yet I feel like I've become spoiled getting to wake up next to you every morning."

He turned around and wrapped his arms around her. "I feel the same way. It's going to be hard going back to sleeping at separate houses again."

"Do we have to?" she asked hopefully.

"Once the situation with Dot has been resolved, we'll be all out of excuses, darlin'." He kissed the top of her head. "You know how it is in small towns, people talk, and I don't want them talking about you."

"I don't care if they talk about me. Besides, I can come up with plenty of excuses starting with the fact that I run a B&B. So far, we've been fortunate that our guests have all been good people, but our luck could change at any minute."

Cole pulled back to look at her. "Are you really concerned about that? I thought you and Molly vetted everyone before accepting their reservations?"

Grace shrugged. "We do the best we can. Whether or not it is a true concern of mine, the answer is yes and no. It is a fear that I have dealt with since the first night Hunter was here. But if I'm being honest, I am using it as an excuse to keep you here."

"Even if we use that as an excuse, what about when you don't have guests staying here?" He pulled her close to him again and gently swayed to a tune they had danced to the night before.

She sighed into his chest as she breathed in his scent. Her experience with men was minimal, but she could not imagine loving anyone else like she loved Cole. And while it would definitely be sudden, she would happily march to the nearest courthouse and marry him on the spot just so she could wake up next to him every morning for the rest of her life. "I'll tell people I'm afraid of the dark," she mumbled.

His laugh rumbled deep in his chest. "Let's not worry about this now, okay? We still have several days together; we can figure it out later."

"Okay," she kissed his chest and reluctantly let go. They had already fallen behind and would have to work extra hard and fast to make up for the loss of time. Grace still needed to get home in time to make breakfast for everyone, and there was a never-ending list of things to do before the rest of the guests arrived tomorrow. Not to mention all the things Cole needed to do. It was worth it, though, these stolen moments. She wouldn't give them up for anything in the world.

They held hands as they walked to their cars. It was a beautiful morning. Sunny and warm, but not too warm, thankfully. She had learned the hard way that there is a big difference between shoveling horse poo in the winter and shoveling horse poo in seventy-degree-plus weather. While they were both gross, one of them smelled bad enough to peel the paint off a car. Unfortunately, that was the one she would be dealing with for the next who knows how many months. You know you're in love when you're willing to subject yourself to that kind of torture on a daily basis.

Not that she was complaining. Cole had offered to get someone else to help on more than one occasion. But Grace had refused each time. Helping with the chores gave her an excuse to see him each morning. Between running the ranch and the bar in town, Cole was so busy they barely had time to see each other. This way, they at least got an hour together each morning. Which was all the more reason she loathed to give up staying with him each night. That hour was sometimes the only time she got to see him.

When the chores were done, they said their goodbyes. "See you tonight?" Grace asked, hopeful the answer was yes.

"Of course, I think I'll leave Jess in charge of the bar again. Tonight is the last night we have together before your guests arrive, and I'd like to spend more time together before things get crazy busy and I have to share you with a bunch of other people."

Grace threw her arms around his neck with an excited squeal. "That's amazing! I'll be counting down the hours," she said enthusiastically.

Cole threw back his head and laughed. "I'm glad to hear it. I was afraid you might be too busy and have to say no."

"I don't think I could tell you no even if I wanted to, which I don't." She kissed him passionately, utterly unaware of how dirty and smelly they were. When they finally broke apart, they both had huge smiles on their faces. "I'll see you later," Grace said as she walked to her car.

"See you later, darlin'," Cole replied.

***

After breakfast, Grace dropped Conor off at the Church for practice and then decided to head over to Bea's Bakery. It had been a while since she'd been downtown, so she was surprised that all the local businesses had decorated for Easter. Despite telling Mayor Allen she would, she still had yet to attend a meeting, so she was woefully ignorant of the town's plans for the upcoming events. Well, ignorant to the parts she wasn't involved in.

She took her time walking up and down the street so she could stop and look at all the window displays. Mr. Wilkins Variety Store displayed colorful Easter baskets, Chrissy's Boutique had Easter morning outfits for the whole family, and even Lula had gotten in on the action with Easter baskets full of eggs spilling over the top. It was not as magical as Christmas, but it was pretty darn close. Even the lamp posts, she noticed, had been decorated, each one alternating between a light-up Easter Bunny and a light-up Cross.

Once she'd circled back to the bakery, she went inside to greet her friend. "You guys have outdone yourselves," she said to Bea, who was busy putting cupcakes in boxes.

Bea looked up and raised her brow. "Oh," she said as Grace's meaning dawned on her. "You must be referring to the decorations. Thank you, it was a tough choice to make. Most of us already had Christmas decorations, so decorating for Christmas was no big deal. But Easter? None of us had decorations for that."

"I know what you mean. I also had to make a special trip up to the city for mine. At least we'll be able to reuse them next year. If we're still doing this...."

"You thinking about quitting," Bea asked curiously.

Grace walked around the counter and grabbed a box. "Why don't I help while we talk. Twenty-four per box?"

"Yes, these are for the classroom parties over at the elementary school this afternoon. Since the kids will be out of school tomorrow, they're having their parties today."

"I forgot about that. And to answer your question, no, I am not considering quitting. It's just, with everything that's been going on, sometimes it's hard to imagine a future with the B&B in it."

Bea gave her a sideways look. "Or would you rather imagine a future with a certain cowboy and some babies in it?"

Grace bit back a smile. "Yes, that does hold a certain amount of appeal, but I'm pretty sure I could do both. I think it's just this whole business with Dot has put a bad taste in my mouth. I'm sure I'll get over it."

A few minutes of silence passed as they filled the boxes. When that was done, Bea sighed as she closed the lid on the last box. "Grace, I don't want to do this, but I need to show you something."

"Okay," Grace replied curiously. "Is something wrong? Has Dot done something to the bakery?"

"No, no, this has nothing to do with Dot." Beas sighed again as she pulled out her phone. "I was working late the other night, and I happened to look outside around the time the bar closes...."

"And?" Grace was starting to get a sick feeling in the pit of her stomach.

"And I saw Cole with another woman. And well, it felt off, so I decided to record it. Here," she said, handing Grace the phone. "See for yourself."

Grace took the phone with shaky hands and pressed play on the small screen. At first, it was hard to tell what she was looking at it; the only light coming from a street lamp several feet away. But then she saw them, Cole and a woman she had never seen before. As far as Grace could tell, Cole did not look very happy. His arms were folded across his chest as he stood silently while the woman did all the talking. Then, all of a sudden, the woman threw her arms around his neck and kissed him.

Stunned, Grace stepped back as if to distance herself from the phone in her hand. Instead, she watched Cole finally push the woman away, both getting in their cars and leaving immediately after. Wordlessly, she handed the phone back to Bea and turned to leave.

"I'm sorry, Grace," Bea called after her.

"Thank you for showing it to me," Grace said as she pushed open the door. "I'll see you later."

Grace drove straight to Cole's. There was no way she could wait until tonight to confront him about the video. Unsure of where he was, she saddled up one of the horses and rode aimlessly around the ranch until she found him in one of the fields. To say he was surprised to see her would be an understatement. He immediately stopped the tractor, jumped down, and ran over to where she was standing, still atop the horse.

"Grace, what on earth..." he stopped talking when he saw her face. "What's wrong?" he finally asked.

"Bea saw you the other night..." she trailed off and watched his face. It became clear the second he realized what she was talking about.

"It wasn't what it looked like, I swear—"

"Who was she?" Grace interrupted.

Cole sighed, removed his cowboy hat, and ran his hand through his unruly hair. "My ex-wife, Valerie. She showed up that night out of the blue. Started talking about getting back together. Guess the grass wasn't greener like she thought it'd be," he said with a shrug.

"I swear, Grace, she kissed me; I did not kiss her."

"What I want to know is why you didn't tell me."

"I was planning to, last night, actually. But then plans changed...and honestly, I forgot. She means nothing to me anymore. I told her to leave and never come back."

Convinced, Grace nodded and turned the horse around. "I'll see you tonight," she called over her shoulder.

"Grace, wait!" he exclaimed. Then, as the horse took off, he grabbed the saddle and pulled himself up behind her. He wrapped his arms around her waist and clasped the reigns bringing the horse to a halt. "You can't come all the way out here and then turn around and leave like that," he said into her hair.

"How on earth did you do that?" she asked.

"Years of practice," he replied.

"You practiced that?" she asked incredulously.

"Not exactly but, why are we talking about this?" he sputtered. "Grace?"

It wasn't easy, but she turned enough in the saddle to look at him. "Look, I know you didn't kiss her, so if you're worried that I think you're cheating on me, you can relax because I don't." He opened his mouth to speak, but she put her finger to his lips. "What bothered me was that you didn't tell me. If you felt like it was something to hide, well, then we would have a problem. But since you forgot..." she shrugged. "I'm willing to accept that and move on."

"Am I allowed to speak now," he asked.

"I suppose I'll allow it."

Instead of speaking, he pulled her to him and kissed her. "You are the only woman I want to kiss. The only woman I want, period." He kissed her again. "I'm sorry I didn't tell you. I would have eventually—"

It was her turn to kiss him, and this time, instead of a quick kiss she kissed him long and hard. When they broke apart, they were both breathless. She laid her head against his chest and listened to his racing heartbeat, sure that hers matched its pace. "Do you think she'll be back?" she asked a few minutes later.

"I hope not, but who knows? I was stunned to see her back the first time. She hated it here. Hated the town, the ranch, the people, even said she hated me."

"I bet she's fallen on hard times," Grace speculated out loud.

"That would make sense. Valerie never worked a day in her life. The man she left me for must have dumped her and left her high and dry. So now she's looking for a soft place to land."

"She sounds charming," Grace said sarcastically. "Anyway, looks like we might have found an excuse for you to keep staying at my house...."

Cole smiled and kissed her again. "Looks like you might be right. So, we're still on for tonight?"

"Of course, I'm making dinner, so I'll see you around six?"

"If not sooner."

Grace turned back in the saddle and turned the horse around. They trotted back to the tractor, and she stopped to let Cole off. Since it had been a while since the horse had been ridden, she let him gallop through the fields to get some exercise. When he was done, she led him back to the barn, where she removed the saddle and brushed him down.

She still wasn't happy about the situation with Valerie, but she had meant what she said when she told Cole she believed him. His body language in the video made it clear he wasn't interested. Unfortunately, the video also made it clear just how beautiful Valerie was. It would be difficult to keep her insecurities at bay, especially since barely two months had passed since something similar had happened with Hunter and Rebekah.

Cole was not Hunter, and Valerie was not Rebekah. But that didn't mean the temptation wasn't there. At one time, Cole had loved Valerie enough to marry her. Had even sworn off women after their divorce. Could Grace really trust that he was completely over her?

-Days till Easter-

Two

Conor walked into the kitchen while Grace made breakfast and sat at the bar. "Anything I can do to help?" he asked.

"No thanks," Grace mumbled absentmindedly.

"Earth to Grace," he said, waving his hand in front of her face. When he got her attention, he put his hand back down. "What's wrong, Grace? You seem very unsettled this morning."

"Sorry about that," she said with a wince. "I'm making blueberry pancakes with bacon for breakfast. Does that sound good?"

"Yes, it does; now, please stop avoiding my questions." When she continued to look at him blankly, he sighed. "Sometimes it's easier to talk to a stranger, you know. Not that I still feel like a stranger, but you know what I mean."

Grace set the bowl of pancake batter on the counter and then turned to face him. "Cole's ex-wife is back in town. She wants him back."

"And does he want her back?"

"He says he doesn't..." she trailed off, suddenly unsure.

Conor raised his brow. "You don't believe him?"

She suddenly felt anxious and started to pace. "Yes, I believe him. It's just—"

"Just what?"

There was compassion in his voice, and Grace wondered if he'd been here before. "She's beautiful. The kind of woman you would expect a man like Cole to be with. So, in other words, the exact opposite of me."

"Grace, come sit down, please," he pulled out the stool next to him and patted it with his hand. She hesitated at first but then finally sat down. "Do you really think Cole is so shallow that the only thing he cares about is how a woman looks?"

Her eyes went wide as what he said sunk in. "I'm being really unfair, aren't I?" she asked quietly.

"Yes, but it's coming from a place of insecurity, not malice. Please trust me on this. Unless Cole has given you a reason not to trust him, do yourself a favor and trust him. The last thing you want to do is give him a reason not to trust you."

"But how would I do that?"

Conor looked away, but not before Grace saw the pain in his eyes. "This kind of thing can tear people apart. If Cole feels you doubt him and his love for you, he will start doubting your love for him. I think the two of you have something extraordinary. Please don't let jealousy or any other green-eyed monster tear you apart."

Grace slowly nodded her head. "You're right. Thanks, Conor. I need to get a hold of myself."

"Yes, you do. And remember, he could have taken her back at the first sign she wanted him. But he didn't. Instead, he came home to you. That should tell you everything you need to know."

She got up and went back to mixing the batter. "I'm very fortunate to have you here to set me straight," she said with a smile. "I hope you'll be one of the guests I keep in touch with."

"I would like that too. Of course, one can never have too many friends. Well, real friends, that is. And who knows, maybe someday we'll even be neighbors."

Grace looked up from the bowl in surprise. "Are you thinking about moving here?"

"Don't tell anyone, but I'm considering it."

"Let me guess, this has something to do with a certain brunette?"

Conor's face broke out in a grin. "It might."

"Does she know you're thinking about moving?" Grace was starting to rethink her stance on two months being too soon to get married. Two couples now have decided to uproot their lives and move to be closer to someone they'd only known for a matter of days. So maybe the saying 'when it's the right one, you just know' is true. Or perhaps they're all crazy.

"We haven't had a chance to discuss it yet. I'm hoping to talk to her tonight after practice. Which reminds me, I won't be here for dinner tonight."

"Oh, that's too bad. The rest of the guests should be here by then, and we're planning to have a cookout and bonfire."

"If I'm back in time, I will definitely stop by."

By the time Grace had breakfast ready, the rest of the gang was seated at the table. Talk turned to the guests and the rest of the work required before they arrived. Molly and Grace still needed to go to the park and hide all the Easter eggs they had stuffed the other day. Emilio and Grant volunteered to help, cutting the time down significantly and giving them time for one more pass with the dust rag.

After breakfast, Grace dropped Conor off at Church and headed to the park. They split the eggs into four large bags, and then each walked off in a different direction with promises to avoid overlapping. The park was large but lacked many good hiding spots, so most of the eggs were going in the grass.

Grace had chosen to go toward the woods to hide her portion of the eggs. As she bent down to place another of the pastel-colored ovals, a flash of white over by the trees caught her eye. Curious about what she saw, she moved closer until she realized that what she had seen was human.

The illusive Dot was back and carrying her own basket of Easter eggs. Beyond tired of dealing with this woman, Grace took off after her and cornered her in a copse of trees. "What's in the basket, Dot?"

"None of your business," she spat.

Grace reached out and yanked the basket out of her hand. Inside the basket were dozens of Easter eggs similar to the ones they were hiding. Inside the eggs, however, was a different story. When Grace opened up an egg, she found it full of gravel. Each one she opened revealed the same thing. "You were going to hide these with the other eggs, weren't you?" asked Grace.

Dot turned her head and refused to answer.

"You hate all of us so much that you would ruin Easter for innocent children? Have you really stooped that low, or have you always been this evil?"

Dot turned to face her, a look of pure disgust on her face. "You gave me no choice. Besides, I'm doing those brats a favor. The sooner they experience disappointment, the better off they'll be."

Grace snorted. "That's pretty rich coming from you, the queen of refusing to accept a little disappointment."

"Whatever, I don't have to explain myself to you."

"No, but you do have to explain yourself to me," said Officer Smith. "Dorothy Stone, you're under arrest." He allowed her to keep her hands in front of her when he cuffed her, but he did lead her away by the arm. The man had been as nice and gentle as possible, but it wouldn't surprise her if Dot tried to claim police brutality. There did not seem to be a low that woman was unwilling to stoop to.

Grace followed them out of the trees and saw Grant standing nearby. He waved his phone at her. "I saw you take off running, so I followed to make sure you were okay. When I saw Dot, I called Officer Smith."

"Thanks, Grant. I owe you one." They watched Officer Smith lead Dot to the back of the police car. "Do you think it's finally over?"

"Yes, I do," Grant said with a nod. "Her son came up from Florida a couple of days ago. He worked out a deal with the local district attorney. Dot will go to Florida with him and into an assisted living facility where they can watch her. She will also be paying a fine to the town and restitution payments to you, Cole, and Gene."

"That's a lot to take in," Grace replied. "Poor Ray, what's going to happen to him?"

"He's thinking about selling his farm and moving to Florida with the rest of his family. I don't know if there's hope for him and Dot, but at least he'd be near family."

"This is all so sad; she had a good life here and threw it all away for what? A reign of terror that ended in handcuffs and a nursing home."

Grant put his arm around her shoulders. "Don't start feeling guilty. Dot brought all of this on herself. You had no control over her choices or her consequences."

"Am I that obvious?" Grace asked as she looked up at him.

"Yes, you are. Now let's get these eggs hidden so we can go to lunch. I'm starving, and this candy is starting to look pretty good."

Grace laughed and headed back toward her section. "Should we have a race?" she called over to Grant.

"You're on. Loser makes lunch!"

***

Grace had lost, but only by one egg. Since the race had been so close, he had decided to treat everyone to lunch at Addie's, something that Grace was incredibly thankful for. There was still a lot to do before the guests arrived, and not having to cook cut down on lunchtime and cleaning up from lunch.

They made it back to the house with just enough time to spare to give the place a quick once over. The doorbell rang at two o'clock, signaling the arrival of the first of their guests. When Grace opened the door, she was greeted by a family of four, Kathy and Ken, along with their sons Avery and Asher. "Welcome, everyone," Grace said brightly. "Come in, and let me show you to your room."

By the time she had led them to their room, the doorbell had rung again. She politely excused herself and ran back downstairs. This time she was greeted by a family of five, Jeff, Sarah, and their kids Leo, Susie, and baby Jewel. Grace hadn't realized there would be a baby in the house and hoped she wouldn't cause any problems. Although all of the guests except one had kids, so, hopefully, they would be understanding.

She settled them in her largest room and got a quick tour in before the next guests arrived. Kimberly, Steve, and their adorable six-year-old twins, Ashley and Abby. That left one more family, Tom and Tia and their daughter Lucy.

While the families got settled, Grace started work on dinner. Since Friday nights were usually the busiest at the bar, Cole was stuck on bartending duty, leaving Grant to man the grill. Not that Grace couldn't; she just couldn't do it all by herself. Cooking for twenty-one was a big deal and one she was still trying to master.

The night started off chaotic, but once everyone had their food, things calmed down. At least as much as they could with eight kids running around. It was the most fun and stressful night she had ever had with a group of guests.

When it was time to make the smores, Grace took over baby duty while Jewel's parents helped her siblings roast their marshmallows. Holding the baby on her hip brought out a slew of emotions, some of which she had trouble identifying. At that point, Cole showed up, and if the look on his face was any indication, his feelings matched her own.

"Who's this?" Cole asked as he let Jewel squeeze his finger.

"This little one is Jewel," Grace replied. "Can you say hi to Cole?" Grace cooed to the baby. Jewel made gurgling noises in return as she squealed in delight at the funny faces Cole was making.

"She's adorable," Cole finally said. "And you look adorable holding her." He kissed Grace on the forehead before taking the baby from her arms.

"I could say the same to you," said Grace. She admired the way he held Jewel in his arms. Trying to stop herself from imagining him with their baby was harder than it should have been. "What are you doing here? Normally you're at the bar until at least midnight."

"I wanted to be here," he said with a shrug.

Grace didn't know how to respond to that. She wanted him here too. But she didn't want him to feel he had to miss work on her account. Jewel started to fuss, so he handed her back to her mom. It was Jewel's bedtime and would likely be the rest of the kid's bedtime soon as well.

The plan had been for the parents to get the kids to bed and then come back down for a happy hour-type get-together, just the adults. However, they were all tired from traveling, so Grace sent them up with their choice of beverage and wished them all a good night.

That done, she set about cleaning up after the fun night. "Can I get you something to eat?" she asked Cole. "We still have some burgers left."

"That'd be great, thanks."

She made him a plate and placed it in front of him at the bar so she could talk to him while she cleaned. "The new guests all seem nice," she said as she wiped down the counters.

Cole ate in silence while Grace cleaned. It was comforting, yet unnerving. They usually had a lot to say to each other. When she couldn't stand the silence any longer, she threw down her rag. "I'm going to bed."

She stomped off toward Granny's room to grab the kitten and then went upstairs, Cole following close behind. When they got to her room, he closed the door behind them and crossed his arms. "Want to tell me what that was all about?"

"I was going to ask you the same question."

"I'm not in the mood for guessing games," he sighed. "I thought you'd be happy to see me."

"I am happy to see you."

"Then why are you standing over there looking like you're ready to breathe fire?"

"I don't know," Grace took a deep breath and let it out slowly. "Maybe it's seeing all those families together with their children. I feel like it brought out some emotions I had buried."

"Emotions from when you were a kid? Or emotions about having kids?"

"Both, I guess. I never got to have experiences like this with my parents. I can't even remember my parents. A part of me has always longed for a family like that."

Cole slowly walked over to her and put his hands on her shoulders. "We could have a family like that. Someday."

"Always someday," she said bitterly. "That's what people have been telling me my entire life. When is someday going to turn into today?"

He pulled her into his arms and hugged her close. "It can be today as soon as you're ready. But this isn't something to rush, sweetheart."

"I guess you're right. But we can at least practice, right?"

His signature, sexy grin spread across his face. "Of course, darlin', we can practice as often as you like."

"In that case," she lifted up on her tiptoes and kissed him passionately. All the feelings she'd been holding back were released through that kiss. It may be too early for marriage and babies, but she could wait. As long as she still had him, that was all that mattered.

-Days till Easter-

One

The morning started off chaotic. Getting four families with a combined eight children out the door and down to the community center for breakfast was somewhat tricky. Even more challenging was making sure those eight kids got something they liked to eat. Apparently, some kids don't like pancakes; who knew?

After breakfast, it was on to the park. The town council had gone all out. There were dozens of food vendors selling every kind of food you could imagine. Booths for face painting, egg decorating, and carnival-style games, and they had even convinced Junior to dress up like the Easter Bunny and pose for pictures with the kids. The park was decorated in festive décor with cutouts of eggs and bunnies everywhere you look.

As one of the festival organizers, Grace was responsible for ensuring everything ran smoothly and putting out fires should they arise. Which basically meant that she spent hours wandering around in case someone needed her. On one of her trips through the main thoroughfare, she ran into Cassie.

"Hey, Grace, have you seen Conor?" asked Cassie.

Grace thought for a moment. "No, I'm pretty sure I haven't seen him since I dropped him off at practice yesterday. Is everything okay?"

Cassie sighed. "We had a talk last night that didn't end well. We were supposed to meet for breakfast this morning, but he never showed, nor is he answering my texts or calls."

That was very concerning. "Let me run over to the house real quick and check on him. I'll let you know what I find."

"Do you mind if I go with you? I'm really worried about him."

Grace hesitated for a minute but ultimately agreed. Since the B&B was only a couple of blocks from the park, they decided walking would be quicker than trying to get one of their cars out of the crowded parking lot. The silence between them lasted less than a minute.

"I'm surprised you haven't asked what our fight was about," said Cassie. "If it were me, it would have been my first question."

"I have a feeling I already know," replied Grace.

"He told you he's thinking about moving here?" Cassie asked in surprise.

"Yeah, he told me before practice. Said he planned to talk to you about it over dinner. I was concerned, but it didn't seem like my place to say something."

Cassie stopped walking, which forced Grace to stop too. "What were you concerned about?"

There were certain times in a person's life when they found themselves in a very uncomfortable position. For

Grace, this was one of those times. It had been years since she had seen Cassie. In fact, she hadn't seen her since high school. Yet, she had heard all about her through the infamous Winterwood grapevine. Of course, that didn't mean that what she had heard was true, but there was usually at least a kernel of truth buried in there somewhere. Now she had to decide how to proceed without offending someone she hoped would be a friend. "I was concerned that it might be too soon to make such a life-altering decision," Grace said carefully.

"And?"

Grace sighed. "And I was concerned that you weren't as interested in him as he is in you."

"That's what I thought." Cassie started walking again and Grace followed along. "I get tired, you know, of people only dating me for my looks. It's been like that since I was a teenager. Never a shortage of men, but never ones who are interested in me as a person. At first, I was offended. Now, I let the guy buy me dinner and a couple of drinks before I bail. People think that makes me a tease and a flirt. I feel it's the least they can do for objectifying me."

"I'm sorry," Grace said apologetically. "I wasn't judging you."

"Everyone judges everyone," Cassie said, waving her hand dismissively. "Some of us deserve it, some of us don't. The thing is, I think Conor is different. I'm just afraid of taking a chance and finding out I'm wrong."

"I think you and Conor have more in common than you think. I won't tell you to give him a chance, but I don't think you will be disappointed if you do."

"At the very least, he deserves my honesty. I just hope he'll be willing to talk to me."

They arrived at Grace's and agreed that Cassie would wait on the porch while Grace went inside to find Conor. His car was still in the driveway, so there was a reasonable chance he was there. Or, at the very least, he hadn't left to go back home. Upstairs, Grace knocked on his door and listened for sounds that someone was inside. Seconds later, Conor popped his head out. "Grace, hi. Is there something I can do for you?" he asked.

"Hey Conor, we missed you at breakfast. Is everything okay?"

"Of course, I guess I just overslept." he ran a hand through his disheveled hair. "Will that be all?"

"There's someone downstairs who would like to talk to you. Are you willing to come down?"

"I don't know, Grace. I'm really not in the mood for company right now."

"I really think you'll want to talk to this person. And if I'm wrong, you can always go back to your room."

"Give me five minutes," he said with a sigh.

"Thank you, we'll be on the porch waiting."

Since Conor hadn't eaten breakfast, Grace threw together a quick platter of fruit, pastries, and a couple of cups of coffee and juice. She took it to the porch where Cassie was waiting and laid it on the wicker coffee table. "He'll be right down," Grace said to Cassie. "Please help yourself; I brought enough for both of you."

Conor appeared, but his expression was more resigned than surprised. "Hey, Cassie," he said. "I guess I should have known it was you."

"I missed you at breakfast this morning," she said softly.

Suddenly feeling like a third wheel, Grace excused herself and left them to talk privately. Five minutes later, she was back at the park. A quick check revealed that all her guests were accounted for and appeared to be having fun. Several were in line to have their pictures taken with the Easter Bunny, several were dyeing Easter eggs, and the rest were either in line for food or sitting at one of the picnic tables.

Grace approached Jeff and Sarah, who were sitting at one of the tables with their kids Leo, Susie, and Jewel. "Are you guys having fun?" she asked everyone.

The older kids nodded between bites of their corn dogs while little Jewel gurgled happily from her stroller. "This has been really nice," said Sarah. "The kids have been having a blast. Unfortunately, this one needs a nap. Do you mind if I take her back to the house?"

"No, I don't, but we're going to start the Easter egg hunt soon. If you think she'll be happy in her stroller, I can take her with me and give you a break?"

"Oh no, I wouldn't want to impose on you like that. You're way too busy for babysitting duty."

"It wouldn't be an imposition at all. I'm just walking around, and if anyone needs me, she can come along."

"You're sure you don't mind?" Sarah asked hesitantly.

"Positive."

"Okay then, thank you so much. It will be nice to spend some time playing with the kids."

Grace smiled at the group, then listened intently as Sarah explained in detail what to do and where everything was in case Jewel woke up. After several reassurances on her part, she and Jewel took off in the direction of the food carts, where they ran into Jake. "Hello, stranger," Grace said with a smile.

"Well, hello there, who have we here?" he asked, peeking into the stroller.

"This little one is Jewel; she belongs to one of my guests."

"Aww, she's adorable!"

"Yeah, she's a good baby. I wasn't sure what to expect with a baby in the house, but she's been a dream. I've had adult guests that whined more than her!"

Jake laughed. "I can only imagine. Where's your other half?"

"Out in the field. You know how it goes."

"Yeah, I do. I've been thinking about talking to Cole about investing in the bar. Since things are getting serious with Evie, I want to become more invested in Winterwood. What are your thoughts on that?"

"Um, I don't know how he would feel about that. I would definitely talk to him about it, though...." Grace trailed off as she spotted Valerie across the park, her mood darkening instantly.

"You look like someone just spit in your Wheaties," Jake said jokingly.

Grace shook her head and tried to shrug off her dark thoughts. "Sorry about that; what were we saying?"

Jake raised his brow. "Want to tell me what that was all about?"

"I just spotted Cole's ex-wife over by the funnel cakes."

"I see; I take it she's back to cause trouble?"

"Seems that way, and I feel like I've already had more than my share as of late."

"If it's not your problem, don't make it your problem."

"Words of wisdom," Grace said with a smile.

Grace and Jake continued talking, only to be interrupted moments later by an angry Valerie who had come stomping over like a bull, ready to charge. "So you're the hussy shackin' up with Cole," Valerie said as she rudely looked her up and down. "Not much in the way of competition."

Grace returned the favor and took in the woman's sky-high red heels, way too short for a family outing, black mini-skirt, and low-cut red blouse. If you could call it a blouse. It looked more like an ace bandage had been wrapped around her several times and tied in the back. She decided to follow Jake's advice and keep moving. "Nice to meet you; now, if you'll excuse us, we're needed at one of the booths."

Not one to take a hint, Valerie followed behind, struggling to keep up since five-inch heels were not made for gravel and dirt. "This isn't over," she yelled behind them. "Cole is mine; it's just a matter of time before he realizes it."

Grace turned back to look at her, smiled and nodded, and then continued on, Jake chuckling beside her. When they managed to walk a ways without hearing from her, Grace turned back to see that she was stopped on the path, trying to pry a rock out of her shoe. "Seems like this might be our chance to make a getaway," Grace said to Jake.

"Let's head over to the field. The Easter egg hunt is supposed to start soon. She'll never make it across the field in those shoes."

They took off giggling like schoolgirls. "I'm glad I ran into you," Grace said when they reached the safety of the field.

"Me too, and remember what I said, okay?"

"I will, thanks."

Jake left to find Evie while Grace hung around to make sure the Easter egg hunt went off without a hitch. They had expected around one hundred kids and planned for one hundred and fifty, which was a good thing since it looked like they were much closer to that number than one hundred.

The kids had a blast looking for eggs, and when Jewel woke up halfway through the event, Grace took her out of the stroller and let her toddle around in the grass. She even found an egg and was so excited Grace didn't have the heart to take it away from her, so she quickly emptied the candy out of the middle and let her play in the sandbox with her new toy.

Six o'clock finally arrived, which meant it was time to go home. These events were a lot of fun but incredibly exhausting, especially for the ones who worked the event. Thankfully, she had planned ahead and already had snacks, appetizers, and a light dinner prepared and waiting at home.

When they got home, she gave Jewel back to Sarah and made quick work of putting out the food buffet-style. Next, the guests would need to take turns using the bathroom, so a rotating schedule was set up based on who was the hungriest. The first chance she got, she went upstairs to check on Conor, only to discover that he and his car were gone. She knew she shouldn't, but she took a quick peek into his room to see if his stuff was still there and breathed a sigh of relief when it was. Hopefully, that meant he and Cassie had made up and were out for the night.

Midnight had come and gone by the time the house had gone quiet, and Cole had come home. "I heard about the incident with Valerie," he said when he walked through the bedroom door.

Grace was exhausted but unable to sleep, so she was up and reading a book by the fireplace. "What about it?" she asked innocently.

"I'm sorry she bothered you. I would love to promise that it won't happen again, but I can't." He kicked off his cowboy boots and climbed into the chair behind her wrapping his arms around her as he settled in.

She set her book on the table beside the chair and turned to face him. "I'd rather not waste precious time talking about her," she said as she pulled his head down for a kiss.

"I knew there was a reason I loved you," he said with a grin.

Grace smacked him on the arm and laughed. "There better be more than one."

"Oh, there is. Perhaps you need a demonstration."

"Perhaps I do."

-Happy Easter!-

"Good morning, baby, Happy Easter," Cole greeted her when the alarm went off.

"Mmm, good morning," she replied. "I can't believe it's finally Easter," she said as she stretched.

"I know what you mean. I'll understand if you need to stay here to take care of things. Your guests need to come first."

"It's okay. If we hurry, we'll have enough time to get everything done. Besides, I want to make sure you can come with us this morning."

They hurried out of bed and over to the ranch. By this point, their routine was well established and ran like a well-oiled machine. They were finished and back at Grace's in plenty of time to get ready for church and get breakfast on the table. Back in the kitchen, Grace got out the bacon along with the ingredients for stuffed french toast.

Despite his offer to help, Grace set Cole up with a place at the counter and a cup of coffee so they could talk while she cooked.

"I forgot to tell you last night," said Cole. "I talked to Jake, and he offered to partner with me on the bar. Said something about trading weekends and having time off."

"How did you respond?"

"Well, I didn't. Before I got the chance, Ray offered to let me buy his farm. He said that since we're neighbors, he wanted to give me first crack at it. Although, it might have been his guilt making the offer.

Grace looked up from the bacon. "Wow, I must admit, I did not see that coming. What did you say to that?"

"I told him I would think about it and get back to him later today. It would be a huge deal for me, Grace, for us. His farm would add another three hundred acres to my ranch."

"That sounds expensive," she replied hesitantly. "I know land around here is cheap compared to other parts of the country, but it can't be that cheap."

"With the deal he's offering, I could afford it. We should tell him yes, and go in on it together."

Grace rolled her eyes. "What is with everyone wanting me to buy property with them all of a sudden? I mean, what is it about me that is giving off millionaire heiress vibes? 'Cause seriously, if I had enough money to buy a farm, I would not be running a B&B."

Cole grinned at her. "You worried I'm with you for your money?"

"Clearly. Honestly, I'm surprised you're not worried I'm with you for yours," she said bitterly.

"Hey," he said, turning her face to look at him. "None of that, okay? I know why you're with me, and money, or lack thereof, has nothing to do with it. Seriously, though, I'm thinking about our future."

"And I'm thinking about your financial advisor who would one hundred percent advise against you involving your broke girlfriend in a large real estate purchase. Even if we were married, it would be risky. Just look at what happened to Ray and Dot, and they were married for over fifty years."

"You're nothing like Dot."

"No, I'm not. But I have a feeling Ray thought Dot was nothing like Dot when he married her," Grace sighed. "I really appreciate you thinking about me, but I don't ever want you to have a reason to doubt my love for you. Or a reason to have to stay with me. If the day comes when we're married and have kids, we can talk about this again."

Cole was silent for a while, so Grace went back to cooking. "I feel like if the roles were reversed, you would feel differently. But I'm willing to let this go for now."

"I feel like you're crazy for bringing it up in the first place. But I'm glad you're willing to see things my way."

"Maybe it was meant to be a gesture of goodwill. Proof I'm serious about this relationship and my commitment to you."

Grace stopped what she was doing again, which, if she ever wanted to get breakfast done, she needed to stop doing. "Is this about Valerie?"

Cole looked surprised. "Why would you think that?"

"Because until she came back to town, we were solid and beyond having to prove our love for each other. Not that she's back, you seem to feel the need to make grand gestures to prove your loyalty."

"It's possible. It would be an unconscious thought, but after everything we've been through lately, I just feel so unsettled. And I guess Valerie isn't helping."

Grace reached across the counter and cupped his face with her hand. "I love you; nothing is going to change that. Dot is gone, and pretty soon, Valerie will be too. Then we can go back to the way things were."

"I don't want to go back to the way things were; I want to move forward—"

"Hey guys," Conor said as he walked into the kitchen. "Am I interrupting?"

"No," Grace said as she gave Cole a we'll-finish-this-later look. "Happy Easter!"

"Same to you," Conor said with a grin. "I'm glad I caught you before the rest of the guests came down. I wanted to ask you a couple of questions."

Once again, she started cooking. "Fire away," she replied as she laid strips of bacon on a cookie sheet.

"Do you know a guy named Tom Adams? He says he works at the high school."

"If you mean Principal Adams, then yes, I know him quite well; why?"

"Oh, he's the principal? That makes much more sense. He approached me after practice last night. Apparently, some of the kids from the play have been talking it up at school, and he's interested in starting a drama program. I guess the kids have been talking about me, so he asked if I would be interested in teaching it."

"Wow!" she exclaimed. "That would be awesome. As you already know, there isn't a lot to do around here besides agriculture-type things, so there are a lot of kids that would benefit from something productive to do that isn't cow tipping."

"I'll second that," Cole said. "The more opportunities the kids have, the better."

"Is this something you'd be interested in?" asked Grace.

"You know what, I think it is. I've really enjoyed my time acting in the play, but I also enjoyed the technical aspects of it. I have such fond memories of my time at summer camp that I would like to give other kids those same memories."

"Would you start next fall?" asked Cole.

"He wants to start this summer. Apparently, their summer school attendance is low, and Principal Adams thinks this would be a good way to raise it."

"So you need to decide quickly then," Grace stated. She put the bacon in the oven and started on the french toast. Stuffed french toast was a favorite among her guests, so she felt confident it would make for a lovely Easter morning breakfast.

"Yeah, I do. Can I stay here for a couple more days? I'll need to get things sorted before I head back home."

"Of course, take as much time as you need. Did you get things worked out with Cassie?"

A huge smile broke out across his face. "We did, and this just might be the sign we're looking for," he said excitedly. "I'll see you guys later. Make sure you come early; I have a feeling it's going to be a packed house."

"Do you want breakfast before you go?" asked Grace.

"No thanks; a woman named Bea is providing donuts for the cast."

Grace smiled at the mention of her friend's name. "I guarantee you won't be disappointed."

With a final wave, he was gone, leaving Grace and Cole alone again. They were just about to resume their conversation when the first of the guests came down for breakfast. After that, it was a whirlwind of feeding the masses and getting them ready to go, the trip to the church just as much of a production as the one to the community center the day before.

When they arrived, Grace saw that someone, likely Conor, had saved several pews for them to sit in. Which was a huge blessing since the church was packed, and there were still twenty minutes to go until the play started. The guests filed into the first two pews, leaving the last one for Grace and her family. She and Cole sat in the middle, with Molly and Grant on Grace's left and room for Granny and Gladys, who had stopped to talk to some friends, on Cole's right. Unfortunately, before Granny and Gladys could arrive, Valerie came slinking in, wearing an outfit a stripper would be proud of and plopped down next to Cole.

Cole shifted closer to Grace's right, which seemed to infuriate Valerie as she, too, moved to the left and practically sat on Cole's lap. Grace was about to unleash one of the seven deadly sins when Gladys and Granny showed up and sidestepped their way into the pew, making a big show out of being elderly and frail and somehow booty-bumping Valerie down to the end of the bench. She would have thanked them from the bottom of her heart if she hadn't been laughing so hard.

As it was, since her plan had failed, Valerie got up and left, which was a shame since out of all the people there, she may have needed to be there the most. Soon after, the lights dimmed, and the play started. Conor was not only a brilliant actor but one of those rare talents who elevated the actors around him. This was supposed to be a small-town church production with only one week to practice, yet Grace could have sworn it was a Hollywood-quality production. Even the kids were so invested in the story that they never once made a peep.

You would be hard-pressed to find a dry eye when it was over. Tissue boxes were passed down the aisles as sounds of people blowing their noses echoed throughout. The play had been hauntingly beautiful, and watching it had been an experience that would stay with her for the rest of her life.

Back home, Grace prepared a large Easter meal of ham with all the trimmings. They had invited Cassie, Evie, and Jake, along with Ray though he had declined. Twenty-six people flowed in and out of the kitchen, some sitting inside at the tables while others took advantage of the beautiful weather and ate outside.

The children, whose energy Grace wished she could bottle up and take each day like a vitamin, were busy running around and letting off some of their pent-up energy from sitting still earlier. This holiday had turned out to be even livelier than Christmas, and Grace was already looking forward to the one next year.

After lunch, Grace pulled out another set of Easter eggs and hid them outside the house. Instead of candy, the eggs contained tokens the kids could exchange for prizes. There were many games, books, and puzzles the kids could choose from, and they could easily be used to entertain the kids on the trip back home the next day. Grace was secretly hoping this would earn her bonus points with the parents since they were the ones who had paid and would leave the all-important review.

While the kids hunted for eggs, the adults stood around talking. Cole accepted Jake's offer to partner at the bar. He would be too busy to run the bar full-time with the new land he would purchase from Ray. This would also give him more time to spend with Grace, something she was thrilled about.

Cassie had been thrilled to hear about Conor's job offer and was on board with him moving to Winterwood. Since Cole was going to have an empty house on his hands once the deal with Ray went through, there was talk that Conor may end up renting it. Which was ironic when you thought about it. Dot had been angry at the prospect of people moving to Winterwood, and now one of those transplants would be living in her old house. If she had just left well enough alone, she would still be home, and Conor could have ended up in Hope Springs like Emilio.

At the end of the day, Cole and Grace retreated to their room, worn out but grateful for the memories of their first big holiday together. "I'm not willing to accept that this is our last night together," Grace said into his chest. They were curled up together on the floor in front of the fireplace.

"You make it sound like we're breaking up," he said as he kissed her hair.

"Feels like it," she said with a shrug. "I can't think of one good reason I should be forced to go back to sleeping alone."

"If you're going to put it that way, then I guess I'll just have to keep coming over."

Grace looked up at him excitedly. "Do you mean it?"

"Of course I do. I love being with you, Grace. I just didn't want people to talk about you, that's all."

"I don't care if they do. Their opinion of me is not worth losing time with you."

Cole gently kissed her lips. "You're sweet, you know that?"

"Not as sweet as you." She pulled herself up to kiss him better and laughed when Ruby, Piper, and Max piled in on top of them. "We may need to give these guys their own room," she said as she gave them all pets.

"The problem is we've spoiled them," he said with a grin. He laughed when Max licked his face with his giant tongue.

They sat that way for a while, petting the animals while discussing the future. It was only a mere twenty days ago when things had seemed hopeless, yet here they were, with a perfect ending to a perfect day.

Afterword

Dear Reader,

Thank you so much for reading Countdown to Easter! I had so much fun writing this book, and I sincerely hope you enjoyed reading it as much as I did writing it. Each book in this series is a stand-alone book, but it is more fun to read them in order. So if you haven't yet read the first two books, check out *Countdown to Christmas* and *Countdown to Valentine's Day*.

For those of you not acquainted with country living, we do tend to complain about going 'up to the city'; we do have a lot of 'elderly' farmers, and they do tend to congregate at the local diner for breakfast in the mornings. None of them, however, are in an elderly gang! At least not that I know of!

My town does not have a B&B, but we have an old railroad hotel like the one they're trying to buy in the book. Of course, any similarities to people or places are coincidental, but I would be lying if I said my real life had zero influence on these novels.

To preview or purchase the next book, and experience more of Winterwood, check out <u>holidaycountdownbooks.com</u>or go to amazon.com and search for the holidaycountdownseries.

Next up will be *Countdown to Mother's Day*, and it's going to be a blast. See how poor Grace copes when not one but two nemeses show up at the B&B along with Hunter and Cole's moms!

Happy Reading!

-Dianna

P.S. Reviews are critical to an author's success, so if you loved the book, please leave a review on Amazon and Bookbub. Thank you so much!

About the Author

Dianna is a wife, mother, reader, writer, and small-town girl at heart. She resides in a rural Missouri town of less than twenty-five hundred people with her husband and three boys in a late 1800s home they've been lovingly restoring when she isn't busy working on her next book.

A romantic at heart, she believes in happily-ever-afters rooted in realism and, most importantly, humor!

She is the author of Forsaking the Dark, a paranormal romance, The Queen's Revenge, a historical romance, and the Holiday Countdown Series, a sweet, small-town romance series.

Made in United States
North Haven, CT
06 April 2025